Not by Chance
but for the
Glory of God

Not by Chance
but for the
Glory of God

J. Jackson

Outskirts Press, Inc.
Denver, Colorado

The opinions expressed in this manuscript are solely the opinions of the author and do not represent the opinions or thoughts of the publisher. The author has represented and warranted full ownership and/or legal right to publish all the materials in this book.

Not by Chance but for the Glory of God
All Rights Reserved.
Copyright © 2010 J. Jackson
v5.0

Cover Photo © 2010 JupiterImages Corporation. All rights reserved - used with permission.

This book may not be reproduced, transmitted, or stored in whole or in part by any means, including graphic, electronic, or mechanical without the express written consent of the publisher except in the case of brief quotations embodied in critical articles and reviews.

Outskirts Press, Inc.
http://www.outskirtspress.com

ISBN: 978-1-4327-5688-8

Outskirts Press and the "OP" logo are trademarks belonging to Outskirts Press, Inc.

PRINTED IN THE UNITED STATES OF AMERICA

Contents

Dedication vii
Not by Chance but for the Glory of God 1
To the Readers of My Story 73
I Love You Grandma 75
I Love You Granny 77

Dedication

*Every Word of this book is inspired by God.
I thank God for every test and every trial,
for without Him I am nothing.*

I dedicate this book to the love of my life. I am so grateful to him for the inspiration that he has been in my life, and I want to share it with the world. I'm sure he never imagined this. I hope that these few words will do justice to what he truly means to me.

My daughter and I have been through so much, and he knows everything about it. He never judged or criticized the choices that I made in my past. No matter how strange the task may seem, he has always been supportive. He is truly my friend. We found our way to each other in the most surprising way. No one matched us up or even suggested we meet. All I know is the very first day he approached me, I knew who he was; I just knew. We fit, just like a puzzle that was meant to be.

The more that I spend time around him, the more I am inspired. He is a genuine person. He believes strongly that people should strive to do what is right, especially people who proclaim to be saints. I admire that quality in him. Being that I have been around the church almost all of my life, I know that everyone who claims to be saved is just simply not. I made it my goal not to have a part in changing his views of anyone. He is dedicated to living saved and serving God. I thank God for allowing us to cross paths.

When I came back home, I was so broken, so broken that I never thought I would get past the trauma that I had endured. I surely never imagined that I would love again. I felt like I was living life from inside a deep, dark hole, and I would never find my way out. Just when I thought that I was content with that, he came along.

When I became the talk of the local church and many others, his feelings never changed for me. I knew that he was special. From the first day he shared with me the feelings stored in his heart, I frequently asked, "Why do you love me?" He would always have a beautiful answer that was somewhat different, every time that I asked. The one statement that remained the same was, "You have a good heart, and I see that."

My love, I want to thank you for looking past every fault that man could dredge up and seeing my heart.

Thank you for teaching me, with the help of God, how to love.

I Love You Always.

Not by Chance but for the Glory of God

- *September 27, 2009, is the day that God impressed upon my heart to start writing a book. Listed below are the thoughts that crossed my mind:*

Here I am thirty years old, divorced, and a single mother of one lovely little girl. She is the best part of the marriage. God gave me a precious jewel, which is the meaning of her name. I am neither angry nor bitter. I am grateful because I am alive and I have the use of a healthy mind. Things could be a lot worse than they are. Through experience I have truly learned that God will never leave or forsake me. He has been with me all of the way. When my burdens became unbearable, God delivered me. I am starting over. I have a cheat sheet now. I know what choices to make, and I also know the choices not to make. I had a firsthand view of the end result of what happens when the wrong choice is made. Nothing happens unless God allows it. The past six years of my life were not His perfect will, but He permitted it. I give Him all the glory and the praise. In honor of my appreciation to God for what He did for me, I choose to tell my story. I will be overjoyed if one young woman or young man reads my story and uses it to his or her benefit by not making the wrong decision regarding choosing a mate. Every Word of God is right. God's Word does not go out void. God's Word does not have respect of person. The Bible says be not unequally yoked with unbelievers. On that note, I will start from the beginning. Here it is.

When I was a little girl, I dreamed and looked forward to the day that I would be a wife and mother. I imagined my husband to be handsome, humble, and a great listener, just like my daddy. My daddy has always been my hero. He has been there for me as long as I can remember. He took so much time with me. As a child, I waited by the door for him to get off work in the evenings. I would climb onto his lap and tell him about all the adventures I experienced in a day's time. He gave me his undivided attention. As I grew toward my teenaged years, this cycle continued. My father helped me verbalize my thoughts.

By the time I reached high school age, I could tell him anything. Sometimes I got frustrated about my circumstances and would not feel at peace until I talked to my daddy. He always knew just what to say. Most of the time, he merely listened. Daddy was very protective of my sister and me when it came to dating young men. We both knew that we would be eighteen years old before we could officially go out. I secretly had some so-called boyfriends. They each had some quality, small or great, that reminded me of my father. He was the first man to show me love; therefore I found myself comparing any others to him.

My parents protected us from the bad things in the world. I didn't understand hurt or how to hurt anyone, because I never experienced that. The truth of the matter is, I never knew or believed that anyone would ever hurt me. I thought that I was in love with the same young man all through high school. We met during my eighth-grade year while I was a cheerleader for my school. He played basketball for his school. We later attended the same high school. He continued to play basketball, and I continued to cheer him on. I could not go out or hang out like the other girls, because my parents would not allow it. Our relationship didn't last long at all. I watched him date many other girls. Every time I saw him with another, it broke my heart again. I believe that he realized how much he was hurting me, so he began to give me a little attention again. All I wanted was to be his "girl" and for him to be the love of my life. He would not commit to me, because we could never spend any time together. My parents had strict rules.

I believed that if I came up with a way to spend more time with him, we could be together again. One particular day I stayed after school for cheerleading practice. I told my mother that practice ended at 4:30. It actually ended at 3:30. This fib would give me an opportunity to walk across the street to the store to spend time with him. By the time I took my seat, my mother walked in the door. She obviously called the school and found out the real time that cheerleading practice ended.

A young woman that lived around the corner from my parents' home befriended me. Everyone kept trying to tell me that she was not my true friend. She wanted something that I had. She was in love with the same young man that I loved. Friends warned that she was getting close to me only to get closer to him. One particular day she planned a get-together at her home. She invited the entire basketball team. She also invited me. I found out later that she promised the young man that I would be there, so he agreed to come. I begged my dad to allow me to go over to her house for a while. I left out the fact that boys would be there. Trusting me, my daddy allowed me to go over for a few hours. Once the team arrived, I was happy, because he and I would have an opportunity to spend time together. We sat and talked a while, watching television. All of a sudden all the boys ran into the house. Seconds later, there was a knock at the door. It was my daddy. He looked at me, and I looked back at him. He said, "Let's go now!"

I got my things, and I was terribly embarrassed as I left the house. It was by far one of the worst nights of my life. I begged my daddy all of the way home to let me go back. I had a feeling that something bad would happen.

The next Monday at school everyone whispered as I walked by. I didn't think anything of it. A young man pulled me aside and told me that my friend was not my friend and neither was the boy that I loved. He told me that minutes after I left that party with my father, my friend and the one I loved went into a room and cut off the lights. Everyone assumed they slept together. I was hurt and disgusted with the both of them. I confronted them separately about the rumor. Both individuals had the same story. They told me that it did not happen. They were only in that room talking.

I wanted to believe them, but my conscience wouldn't allow me to rest. I began to replay events and ponder what the people who loved me were saying. They all had my best interest at heart. They had no reason to want to see me hurt. Finally a long-time friend of my family came to me and made me see the truth. I was like a sister to the person, and he was furious with my so-called love. I finally saw the light about the girl around the corner. Because I am so big-hearted, I forgave her, but my relationship with her was never the same. As for the young man, I forgave him too. He was my first love, and I could not stop feeling the way that I did for him at that time.

Later, another young woman in school ended up pregnant, claiming that her child was his child. He was proven to be the father. My feelings for him began to grow cold. I could not look past his having gotten a girl pregnant. He soon graduated from school, and I became a senior in high school. While he was away at college, I realized that boys other than him existed. I could have fun just like any other girl my age.

As I heard about the women my so-called boyfriend dated while in college, I entertained a couple of other young men at our high school. Neither situation worked for me. I began to focus more on God. I was about to start my life as a young adult. In the midst of all of the drama in high school, I maintained good grades. I was accepted into a four-year university. It was time for me to get serious about my future.

I was faithful to our local church and district. I began to be faithful to the jurisdictional church services, also. I went to choir rehearsal one night, and I saw him. He played the organ quite well, and he seemed sweet. I looked at my younger sister and I said, "He is the man that I am going to marry." She smiled at me.

I continued to go to rehearsals. We had rehearsal every month. Any time I was in his presence, I felt him watching me. We talked and introduced ourselves one particular night. We exchanged phone numbers. We began to call each other and talk on the phone periodically. Those phone conversations increased in frequency. We went on several dates, to the movies and out to dinner. My senior prom came around, and I asked him to go with me. He told me that going to proms went against what he was taught. He told me that I should go and have fun. I contemplated it, but I could not go without him. I could not imagine another gentleman on my arm; therefore, we went out to eat and had a great time, while my friends enjoyed their senior prom.

We dated for nearly three years. It didn't take him long to steal my heart. I was very active in my church, and he was very active in his. My father was my pastor. His father was his pastor. The closer that we got, we both recognized that there was a problem between us. He loved his church and was dedicated to it. I loved my church, and I was loyal to my father.

One day he asked, "Can you ever see yourself leaving your church?"

I asked, "What do you mean?"

He explained, "If your husband wanted you to go, would you?"

I said, "Yes, that is the way that I have been taught." I gave him the answer that sounded good. Because of my upbringing, I would comply.

Deep down, he knew that leaving my church would tear me apart. He recognized the close bond between my father and me. I felt that my father needed my support at our church. I taught Sunday school, tried to play the organ, worked with the choir, and sometimes taught the weekly youth class. Next to my mother, I believed that I was my daddy's biggest fan. Every word out of his mouth was like gold to me. I enjoyed when my name appeared on the program as the soloist before he went up to speak.

I love my daddy. He has always been my hero, and I believed that I would always be his little girl. As much as I avoided the fact, leaving my church would destroy me, because I thought it would destroy my daddy.

All my closest friends were getting married, one by one. They were older than me. I began to desire to be married also. I thought about it constantly. I know that there are many other young women who can relate. I wasn't ready mentally, financially, or spiritually to be anyone's wife. The Word teaches us that whoso finds a wife finds a good thing and obtaineth favor with the Lord. That was my problem. A husband should have been finding me. I was so focused on my friends and their marriages that I wanted to be married too. I tried to hide it from the boy I was dating, but he saw straight through that. I went as far as to name our children. I even told him the time frame in which he and I would be married. In so many words, I gave him an ultimatum.

Our relationship went downhill from there. We couldn't go any further. I wanted to be married so badly, but he acknowledged the fact that neither of us were ready. To me, he was the responsible one. I opened a door, and he walked out of it. I told him that we should take a week off and pray and seek God for an answer as to where we should go from that point. A week passed. It was one of the hardest weeks of my life. On the seventh day, I patiently waited for a phone call from him. When he hadn't called by nightfall, I called him. I could hear in his voice that the answer wasn't what I was hoping and praying for. He told me that God didn't tell him anything regarding us, so maybe we should go our separate ways. I agreed with him. I felt that if he were the one for me and I was the one for him, we should know. We decided that day to end our relationship. We did not speak to each other conversationally for nine years.

I was very hurt. I had planned my future around being married to that young man. I wondered what direction I had to take next.

I cried for two weeks. I thought I could hide that from my customers. An older gentleman spotted me, though, as I worked in the drive-through window at the bank. One day, while waiting on customers, I received a phone call. The man's voice on the other end of the phone said he noticed I had been sad for a few days. Later that week, I received a dozen roses from him. He called the bank every day to tell me how beautiful I was. He also told me that he wanted to see me smile again.

My father taught me to turn to God for strength while hurting. For some reason, I did not. All I had to do was look to Jesus, the author and finisher of my faith. Not one time did I ask Him to help me; neither did I ask for direction I did not need anyone to tell me this. My parents modeled this in their everyday lives. I was a grown woman. I knew to lean on my heavenly father. I thought that I could get through my pain my way.

I entertained the man on the other end of the phone. He gave me attention, which made the pain not hurt so bad. That experience showed me firsthand that the devil studies us. He knows our weaknesses. The man figured out that I needed someone to listen me, like my daddy. We exchanged phone numbers, and he listened to me talk about my hurt and pain nonstop. Talking about it made me feel better. I should have talked to God.

The man kept sending flowers and coming by the bank and offering me money. He soon realized that things did not impress me.

Even though I was grown and in college, my daddy was good to me. He told my sister and me that nothing was free. He told us never to take gifts from men, because they always wanted something in return. My father told us we should ask him for what we want. If he couldn't buy it, or we couldn't work to get it ourselves, then we did not need it. I remembered that. My father kept up his end of the promise. Whatever I needed, he found a way to get it for me. I never had to depend on a man for anything.

Those flowers kept coming. They made the bank look beautiful, because I could not bring them to my daddy's house. The only thing that kept me from falling in this trap and giving in to the man's advances was the fact that I remained faithful to God.

Even though I didn't understand the importance of developing a relationship with God, I kept going to church every time the doors opened. Therefore, God could help me, even when I did not realize that I needed help.

Before I knew it, that friendship ended and the man was out of my life before he had a chance to walk in. I later found out that he was married and hiding that fact from me. One day some of his coworkers came into the bank. His name came up. One of the people who worked with me asked, "Is he married?"

All of his coworkers answered, "Yes." They looked at me and laughed.

One man replied, "You really didn't know, did you?"

I looked up and thanked God. A couple of months passed, and I began to say frequently, "I don't need a man. I am going to enjoy myself. I tried dating the Christian way, and I was hurt. I no longer care. I want to have fun like my other girlfriends."

I was sitting at my teller window when a man walked up and stood in front of me. He was dressed in old dirty clothes. He appeared to be older than me. He looked at me and said, "You are such a beautiful person, inside and out."

I said, "Do you know me?"

He said, "Yes."

I asked, "How?"

He said, "I can't tell you." He told me that it would scare me if he did. That man told me that I would have beautiful children. He said, "As a matter of fact, your first child will be a girl. She will look just like a little angel. Everywhere she goes people will always tell her how beautiful she is."

I begged and assured this man that he could tell me how he knew me; that I would understand. I wanted him to know that I knew God and I believe in the power of God. The man immediately left. I walked away from my teller window and looked all over for him. I could not find him anywhere. In my heart, I felt that I had entertained an angel. Someone had told me days before that happened that because children loved me so much, I would never have kids of my own. That statement discouraged me. God sent a messenger to encourage me. I did not think about my encounter with that angel until six years later.

Things at the bank started getting better. I was feeling like my old self again. My manager gave me a Friday off. I had previously ordered some rims for my car. The rims were due in on the following Monday. The salesman from the store called and told me that my rims were in. As I sat and watched a soap opera, I contemplated waiting to get my rims done on Monday as planned. My first thought told me to wait until Monday. I went to the rim store anyway. I lived by the creed, "Don't put off for tomorrow what you can do today."

As I parked my car, making ready to enter the store, I felt him watching me. He watched me as I walked across the parking lot. He watched me as I bent over to pick up the keys that I dropped. I signed in and took a seat in the waiting room. I asked if anyone was watching TV. All of the people said, "No," so I proceeded to put the TV on the soap opera that I liked to watch. After a while, no one was left in the room but that man and me. He asked my name. He told me that his name was Ethan. I immediately blew him off by informing him that I had a boyfriend. He assured me that he was merely trying to make conversation, not take me on a date. I laughed and calmed down enough to have a conversation with him. I told him that he looked very familiar to me. He shared that he had a younger brother who attended the same college as I did. I looked at him and instantly realized that I knew his brother. His younger brother dated one of my classmates.

One particular day in class a group of girls were sharing stories. I heard a story about a young man who had been in a bad accident. He was hurt very bad and he barely survived. Three women showed up at the hospital claiming to be his wife, because the doctors allowed only immediate family in to see him. I laughed as I thought, "He must be a bad man."

BACK TO THE RIM SHOP

We continued to talk. He told me that he had been in a terrible accident a few years before. His story brought tears to my eyes. I was completely blown away. I asked, "Are you saved? Are you in church?"

He said, "Oh, Lord."

I said, "Well if God had spared my life the way that He has yours, I would be breaking down the church doors praising Him."

He said, "I tried to go to church, but the churches back home are not right, especially the preachers."

I yelled, "Excuse me!" He shared that he had zero confidence in men of God because he knew them to be womanizers, and he knew women personally who experienced this from the last preacher that he attempted to give a chance.

I shared with him that my father is a preacher and God leads him as he leads us. I said, "He is saved and is unlike the people you are describing."

He asked, "What is the name of your church?"

I told him, proudly. My personal mission became to show the young man that God is real and that there are people out there who really live according to the Word of God.

Soon the salesman came into the room and told him that his car was ready. My new acquaintance told me that he did not feel comfortable leaving me there by myself. He asked me to ride with him to the mall down the street while the people at the store finished working on my car. I felt that it would be okay. Against my better judgment, I took a ride.

I walked in a shoe store and admired some sneakers that I had been watching for quite some time. Ethan suggested that I try them on. Once I had the shoes on my feet, he told the clerk that he would purchase them for me. I seriously considered taking the gift. I really wanted those shoes. I remembered the advice from my father. I got paid in a couple of weeks and I could buy them at that time.

I took the shoes off my feet and handed them to the clerk. I told Ethan that I could not accept a gift such as that from him.

He asked, "Why?"

I explained that I gave my daddy my word that I would not. I told him that my daddy told me not to take gifts from men. If I can't buy it myself, my father would buy me what I wanted and needed. He assured me that I could have the shoes, no strings attached. I said, "No."

He looked at me and said, "You can't be for real."

After leaving the shoe store, he took me back to the rim shop to pick up my car. I felt bad about snapping at him earlier. Before getting out of the car, I apologized to Ethan. I confessed that I really did not have a boyfriend, and I just got out of a relationship. I explained, "I am still hurting, and I am not looking for anything serious." We exchanged phone numbers and went our separate ways.

He lived a couple of hours away. He came to visit once a week. We went to see all the movies that came out.

I lived with my parents at that time. I decided to get an apartment with two other girls. Ethan's visits began to increase. The more the visits increased, the guiltier I felt. That is one positive characteristic about myself that I've always thanked God for. I have an out-of-this-world conscience.

Ethan was nice to me. The more time that I spent with him, the more I wondered, "Am I falling in love with this man?" In the beginning, we both agreed, "no strings." I was having fun.

My family planned a trip. Ethan insisted on seeing me before I left. I had so much to do that I begged him to wait until I returned. He insisted upon visiting anyway. As soon as I sat across from him at the restaurant, I saw it. It was a hickey planted on the side of his neck. I thought, "It couldn't be."

He saw me looking at it and told me that he was working in the yard and a wasp bit him. I was angry at him, more so because he lied to me. I asked him to take me home. I went on my trip with my family, and I did not accept any calls from him the entire time. I was hurting because I missed him.

When I returned home, all my friends wanted to know how things were going with Ethan. I told them the wasp story. His new nickname became "Wasp." As everyone joked about it, I cried on the inside. I truly liked him. He kept calling, and I kept ignoring him.

I talked to a close friend of mine, and she reminded me that I couldn't officially be angry at him because I started the "No-Strings-Attached Rule." I was hurt because he disrespected me and he lied.

One day he called, and I decided to talk to him. He apologized and admitted that it was really a hickey. He told me a long, drawn-out story about how his ex-girlfriend cornered him in the post office and got angry at him when he told her about us. She grabbed him and planted the hickey on his neck. I forgave him, and we started to date again. This time we agreed to officially have a relationship.

I Should Have Stayed Away

He called all day every day. We spent every free moment together when I wasn't at church, work, or school. The relationship was going well. He came to visit one day, and he took me to meet his mother. As we walked to meet her in the front yard, he said, "Mom, this is the woman that I am going to marry." That was like music to my ears, because deep down, I wanted to be married. He talked about his daughters all of the time and how much he loved them. He brought them with him to visit on many occasions. He and his oldest daughter had such a close relationship that it reminded me of the one that I share with my daddy. He would frequently say, "I wish that you had not left me for two months."

I would ask, "Why do you always say that?"

He never answered, but one day he said, "I have something to tell you. I have a son, but his mother won't let me see him." Ethan proclaimed that all he ever wanted was a son. It hurt him to know that his son lived in the same city as him and they could not have a relationship.

I felt sorry for Ethan as tears formed in his eyes while telling me this story. After a while, Ethan started spending time with his son. He brought him to meet me. In the beginning Ethan's son did not like me. I have a special love for all children. It became my mission to win the child's heart. It took some time, but the young man grew to love me as I him. I loved all of Ethan's children, because they were a part of him.

I Did Not Expect Another

Ethan and I became closer and closer. His visits became more frequent. He asked me to ride to his house with him one particular day. It was two hours away away. I kept telling him that it seemed that he had something to tell me. He couldn't find the words until the trip back to my house. He said again, "You shouldn't have left me for two months."

I said, "Okay, please tell me what happened. Is someone pregnant?'

He said, "The baby isn't here yet, so I don't want to talk about it." He told me that the young woman was six months pregnant. I was hurt, but I convinced myself that I should not hold it against him, because were we not together when the child was conceived. I told Ethan that I needed some time to think about this new piece of information. In my heart, I didn't think I could deal with it. He begged me to stay with him. I told him that the situation surrounding the child would forever be a problem for us while we tried to build a relationship. He convinced me that it would not. He would not allow it to be. He shared with me his desire to be a good father to his child; that was it.

The baby was born.

Ethan fathered a beautiful baby girl. He brought her with him on many of his visits. This was very new to me, somewhat exciting.

I gave him permission to allow her mother to call and check on her while she was at my house, because their hometown was so far away. She called many times when he was there. The situation appeared to be working itself out. He and I were a couple, and the two of them were being parents to their child.

My family planned a barbeque. Ethan promised me that he would be there. I looked for him and waited. He never showed up. Finally he called and told me that there was a small problem. He said that his new baby's mother was in need of a place to stay. He could not help her financially, so he offered to allow her and her children to move in with him temporarily. He stated, "I cannot have my child living on the street."

In my supportive nature, I encouraged him to be there and do what he must. I cried the rest of the day from disappointment. My little sister patted me on the back and told me that God was in control of all of this. She said, "Ethan is not worth it. Lately, you are always sad."

I knew that God was speaking through her. I knew in my heart that Ethan was bad news. I loved him. I always wanted to believe the best concerning him. I could hear God speaking, but my flesh was speaking louder.

Ethan was working hard to convince me that nothing was going on between him and his baby's mother. He told me that she and the baby slept in his bedroom, and he slept on the couch. He and I talked on the phone every day and night. He assured me the living arrangement was temporary. He began to tell me that he couldn't stand being there. He spent most of his time visiting me. He went to church with me, even choir rehearsal. It seemed that he did anything to avoid being at home. One particular day, he brought the baby with him. He said that we would take the baby home as soon as her mother got off work. The baby's mother got off at three o'clock. We arrived at her job at that time and took the baby to her. She came outside very angry. At the time, it did not dawn on me why.

We drove back to my house and enjoyed the rest of the day. He later arrived back at his house to find an empty home. She and the baby had left. She had thrown all of his food from the cabinets and the refrigerator in the front yard.

He always assured me that he and this young woman were friends and they were working to be parents to their child. What I could not understand was the source of her anger. I tried to be supportive of him; I believed whatever he said.

Things began to settle down for Ethan and me again. He told me that he wanted to be with me all of the time. He asked me how I felt about moving to his hometown. I told him that the only way that I could imagine living there was if he and I were married. He gave me a spiel about living together first to get to know one another.

I proclaimed, "Out of the question!"

He began to frequently talk about and make reference to our being married. He knew that I wouldn't have it any other way. I could not disrespect my parents by living with him without being married. I resented the fact that he asked me to consider it.

Ethan decided to get a part-time job to save money. His visits decreased. One particular weekend, I did not hear from him at all. I worried about him because I did not get any answers when I called. I drove all the way to his house. When I arrived and saw his truck parked in place, I cried all the way home, because I had a feeling that our relationship was in trouble again. Later that same night, I received a call from a different girl claiming to be Ethan's girlfriend. She told me that she had been with Ethan, and they worked together. She shared that he gave her rides to work. She got my phone number from his caller ID. She then called the baby's mother on a three-way call. They had previously been on the phone before I was called. They both claimed to be involved with Ethan. There I was, hurt and disappointed again. I made up in my mind that I was through with him.

I heard a voice say, "You love him; you are going to look stupid if you don't see this through." I did not call him. I just waited and ignored his calls. Deep down, I wanted an explanation. I didn't know either of those women. They were not friends to me. They did not have my best interest at heart.

The next time he called, I answered and listened. He began to talk as if nothing happened, rambling on about having a rough weekend and needing time to himself. I just listened. When he finished rambling, I inquired about the girl who called me. He told me that she was a young girl just out of high school, and he was doing her mother a favor by giving her a ride to work. Their car was not working. He apologized for not telling me about her sooner. He acknowledged the fact that she had a crush on him. He didn't think that she would do anything like call me with a lot of lies.

I told him that the baby's mother was in on the conversation too. I learned that there is more between the two of them than being parents to their child.

He explained that both women were jealous because he chose to be with me. He said, "They hate each other, but they became friends to destroy our relationship."

I remembered that they had a few negative words with each other while on the three-way call. I believed him. My questions list as follows: "What is the big deal about him? Why do so many women want him?" It never dawned on me that he was giving them reasons to be angry. I kept trusting him. God was yet dealing with me. Even when I ignored, I could hear a still voice speaking. Everything about the relationship was wrong. There were many red flags and stop signs. When I would not hear God, He sent messengers. They would say the same things that I could hear God saying. I turned a deaf ear to the voice of God. I had a big heart. I felt sorry for the baby's mother. She had a newborn baby by him, and she was trying to be a good mother to her other children also. She needed Ethan. I did not.

He tried to talk me out of my thoughts. He was convinced

that she, along with other women, wanted him badly because of money. He felt that what we had was love.

I knew about his financial situation. I was also aware that he was about to come into a lump sum of money. I could see his point. I know that money makes people do crazy things, but at the same time, I felt bad for his baby's mother. I made a decision that I was going to take myself out of the relationship so that she could have him.

I called him on my way to work and told him about my decision. He told me that if I didn't want to be with him, it was fine. He said, "I won't be with her."

I said, "We will finish this when I get off work." I entered the door, and the assistant manager called me into his office. He told me that he received a call from a woman claiming to be Ethan's wife. She shared her concerns about my calling their home from the work phone at times I should be working. She suggested that he check the company's phone records so that he could see how much Ethan and I talked during work. He told me that he knew the woman wasn't Ethan's wife. He said, "You have a vicious enemy, and she wants to get you fired." God gave me favor with people. He told me not to worry. I was a good employee, and my job was secure.

I was angry. I was about to give up the man that I loved to this woman. I called and told Ethan what happened. This helped his case. He was on a mission to prove that his baby's mother was evil. This was ammunition in his favor.

There were things that I overlooked. The only way that she could know that I was calling him from work was because she had been in his house with access to his caller ID.

I thought that I was in love. I was walking through life wearing rose-colored glasses. This was not love. It was stupidity. I kept ignoring the feelings that I had about this relationship being wrong. My church members kept coming to me one by one, encouraging me to seek God about marrying this man.

God allowed the closest woman to me to have a dream about

him. She dreamed that he was sneaking in and out of the back door of her childhood home. She not only shared the dream with me, she interpreted it. She told me that it meant that he had a problem with women. One woman would never satisfy him. She told me that she loved me and she would support my decision. She said, "I am praying for you."

I felt so much pressure. I felt like the walls were caving in on top of me. I thought, "We love each other. If we just get married, all will come together."

I received a call from Ethan's brother. He said that he was about to go to visit Ethan. Ethan's brother thought that Ethan was in trouble. He asked me to ride to Ethan's house with him. As we got closer and closer to the house, I began to feel sick to my stomach. We arrived there to find that Ethan had been arrested and released. His baby's mother called the police on him for raping her. Ethan explained that he told her that he was about to come and visit me. She said, "If you leave, I am calling the police." She previously told him that something was wrong with the baby, so he came over to check on his child. When he told her that he was leaving, she got angry. She later went to the police station and dropped the charges. Ethan was tired of all of the drama and so was I, sick and tired! She decided that she no longer wanted to see Ethan and me together. He told me that for the sake of peace, I should not come with him anytime he was to go around his child's mother. I agreed, because it seemed that anytime that he encountered her, it turned into a chaotic situation. He promised me that things would go back to normal after we got married.

On our wedding day, one of my very best friends came out in the hallway as I was preparing to enter the church. She looked at me and began to cry. She hugged me and went back in the church. I cried all the way down the aisle. It finally hit me that I was making the wrong decision. I wanted to get on the microphone and apologize to everyone for wasting so much time and money. I did love him. I knew that once I made this step, I couldn't turn back. We said, "I do."

What Have I Done?

Once we made it to our destination on our wedding night, my friends had decorated our room. I was excited. Ethan looked at all of the decorations and went and got in the bed. I got out of the shower, and he was sound asleep. I went to sleep also. We woke up the next morning and rode to our home. We had a happy marriage for approximately two weeks. I returned to my hometown one night to go to church. I went to a jurisdictional meeting at which our Bishop was the speaker. He spoke a Word from the Lord just for me. In his message out of nowhere he said, "God's Word does not go out void. It has no respect of person. The Bible says, "Be not unequally yoked with unbelievers." The Bishop said, "If you go against His Word, it will not work. I don't care who you are!"

That Word hit me hard. If it were a knife, I would have bled to death right there.

That same weekend, Ethan's children spent the night with us. Ethan went downtown to ride around, which he liked to do on weekends to showcase his latest vehicle. This particular night the children and I stayed home. I allowed them to lie in the bed with me until he came home. When he came home, he slept on the couch. I was angry when I woke up the next morning and did not find him in the bed with me. I previously explained to Ethan how important it was for a husband and a wife to sleep in the same bed every night possible. I shared my feelings about it when we were alone. That conversation turned into an argument. Ethan made it clear that I was overreacting. We did not share the same feelings about this.

Ethan purchased a car for me. It was my very first brand-new car. I wanted to be a blessing to a very good friend of mine; therefore I gave her my old car. My old car was special to me, because it was the first car that I completely paid for on my own. My friend was special to me also. I knew that she would appreciate that car as much as I did.

I liked the new car, but it wasn't what I wanted. It was a car that Ethan picked for me. It cost twice as much as the one that I wanted. I did not understand why he was so persistent on thinking for me and giving me what he thought I should have. It was a new car, so I didn't complain.

After being married a week and a half, Ethan shared with me that he was ready for me to have a child. I explained to him that there was so much that I wanted to do first. I really wanted us to enjoy being married for a while and truly get to know one another first. I took my birth control pills faithfully before going to bed.

One day I searched the house, and I could not find my pills. I asked Ethan if he had seen them. He shrugged and talked about his wish to have a child now. After he continually watched me search and search for my pills, he admitted that he took them. He then forced me to be with him, and I cried the entire time. I had missed two nights of taking my contraceptives. I knew what was inevitable. When the time approached for my monthly visitor, I showed no signs. There were no cramps, no bloating, or anything. The time came and went. My monthly visitor never came. I took three at-home pregnancy tests. They all showed the same result. I was expecting a child, ready or not.

The following weekend Ethan made arrangements to see his youngest child. As he prepared to take her home on Sunday, he asked if I wanted to go with him. I hadn't been around his baby's mother in a long time. It seemed that when I stayed away, Ethan and I had peace. My conscience led me to take the drive with my husband. Being the supportive wife that I thought I should be, I told him to go without me this time. This cycle continued. He never asked me to ride with him to pick up this child again. He went alone.

One particular day I told him that he broke his promise to me. He refused to allow me to ride with him to pick up this child. His reasons involved his not wanting to upset the child's mother. I felt disrespected, because I was his wife, and there he was blatantly putting another woman's wishes before mine. We exchanged words, and then it happened. He grabbed me, and like it was second nature, he slapped me across the face. I dropped to the floor on my knees and cried. I reminded Ethan that he promised me that he would never hit me. He held me and apologized. While he was apologizing, Ethan tried to convince me that he did not actually hit me. He said that he was trying to grab my shirt, and my face ran into his hand. It didn't take long for him to convince me. I believed whatever he said. I consistently stared at the red mark on my face. I bruised easily. I covered it with makeup until it faded away on its own.

Before Ethan and I were married, my father told Ethan that I always had a home. He asked Ethan never to put his hands on me. My father said, "I love her, and I will always want her. If you ever hit her that tells me you no longer want her. Send her home to me." Ethan gave my father his word that he would never have to worry about that. I reminded Ethan that he broke his promise to my daddy, but Ethan kept saying that he did not hit me. It was an accident.

I began to accept the fact that I was having a baby. As a child, I always fantasized about dressing up my little girl and being a good mother to her. For some reason, I lost sight of what I wanted. I lost myself in what he wanted. Ethan had mostly girls and one boy. His desire was to have another son; therefore, I wanted a son too. I bought all blue maternity clothes. I just knew that it would be a boy. God used a very good friend of mine to speak into my future. She gave me a Word straight from God. She said, "God says you are having a girl, and she will be a company keeper for you." I knew that God used my friend mightily. If she said that God showed her something, I knew that He did. I wanted to please Ethan so badly that I put aside what I wanted.

I went to the doctor regularly, as prescribed. My mother went with me on the day that I was to find out the sex of my child. I heard the nurse say clearly, "She is so busy." I already knew in my heart that my baby was going to be a girl. The nurse saw the disappointment on my face. She told me that she wasn't really sure, and she could be wrong. Her instincts said it is a girl.

It took a while, but I accepted the fact that I was having a girl. Ethan seemed happy too, after a while. I picked a beautiful name for her; it was going to be Taylor Jená. I wanted to give her a part of both of my parents' names. This meant so much to me. When Ethan found out that it was a girl, he told me that I could name her. He didn't care. I labeled all of her things. I shopped for her and dreamed about her. I couldn't wait for the day that she would be born. I was very happy about my baby girl.

Ethan and I were doing okay, as long as his youngest child and her mother weren't mentioned. They were sore subjects for us, and everyone involved knew it. He mentioned going to pick up his daughter. He said that her mother didn't want me to come with him. She couldn't bear seeing us together. I told him that I wasn't sure how long I could keep this up, because it was too disrespectful to me as his wife. Ethan told me that things had to be that way, and he wasn't going to do anything about it. He said, "If you don't like it, you know where the door is." I was pregnant with no job. What was I supposed to do?

Ethan came home and told me that his three daughters by his ex-wife were going to move in with us for a while. He said that their mother was having a hard time, and she asked him to come and get them. The arrangement was that she would keep them on the weekends, and we would keep them during the week.

They moved in, and Ethan enrolled them in school. I really didn't know how to cook. I was learning, but I tried. I had to make sure that we had dinner. I had three heads to comb daily. I had to help with homework. I became a full-time mother, ready or not. On top of that, I was pregnant. I was not enjoying married life at all. This was not what I dreamed it to be.

Ethan came in one day and mentioned that he and the kids were going to pick up his youngest daughter. I rolled my eyes. There was always tension between Ethan and me because of the situation with the youngest daughter and her mother. The kids knew it. They didn't mention the situation.

I felt that Ethan, his baby's mother, and his kids were a family. I was just there being used. Ethan yelled, "I am sick of your attitude." He grabbed me by the arm and slung me across the dining room floor. I cradled my stomach with my arms to protect the baby as I rolled across the floor. I had just fixed all the children's plates for dinner. The children were all sitting at the bar eating. One of the girls screamed. The oldest one put her head down. The other one cried. I knew that I didn't fall on my stomach. In my heart I felt that my baby was okay. I couldn't believe that Ethan had thrown me around like that, especially in front of the children. It was hard for me to face them after that happened.

The more often that Ethan belittled me in front of them, the less I wanted to be around. Ethan later apologized for his actions. As usual, I forgave him. There was no pain or bleeding. I assumed that Baby Taylor was okay.

I went shopping and bought many beautiful maternity clothes. Dressing up made me feel beautiful. The bigger I got, the less attractive I was to my husband. People told me I was beautiful pregnant. Ethan made me feel hideous.

Before the children came to live with us, Ethan frequently stayed out overnight. He claimed to need time to himself to clear his head. I honestly looked forward to his trips away, because it gave me opportunities to go to my parents' home and spend time with my family. I felt like my husband did not love me or no longer found me attractive. He was distant all of the time.

Ethan found out that the mother of his three girls was expecting a child. He was so angry that he pulled them out of school and took them back to her. He said that he was helping her out to make her situation better. If she had time to make another child, she could raise the three she had. I must admit, there were a lot of problems in our marriage. Our home was not a stable place for those children. Ethan was abusing me in front of them, which was not healthy for three growing girls to witness.

When Ethan took the girls back home, he began to disappear again. This time I marked the dates of his trips on my calendar. They occurred once a month. One particular time, he called to tell me goodnight. He said that his phone wasn't working and his charger was in the truck. He would have to call me in the morning. I said, "Give me the number to your hotel room, so I can call you if I need to."

He refused, claiming that the front desk could not turn the phone in the room on for him.

At that point I said, "Enough is enough!" I went to our house and packed my things, pregnant and all. Not only did the man have the nerve to abuse me, but he was also cheating.

When he came home and found my things gone, he called and assured me that nothing was going on. He really needed time to himself. It helped him deal with stress. He persuaded me to come back home. I never saw him do anything with my own two eyes. I did not have real proof of his cheating, so I thought I had no real reason to leave.

Things got better for a little while. I was getting bigger by the day. I couldn't ignore the fact that something was going on with Ethan, though. He slept with his phone connected to his hip. It rang all day long. He would look at it and not answer. He would tell me, "It is the wrong number."

I couldn't wait until I had the baby. I felt that I wasn't attractive to him anymore, since I was pregnant. I went to visit my parents, and I began to have contractions. My mother took me to the hospital. I was in labor, and it was too soon for the baby to come. The doctor stopped the contractions and sent me home.

I knew that all the stress wasn't helping me, so I focused again on the baby. I had to stay healthy for her. The nurse in the emergency room encouraged me to do whatever it took to keep that baby with me as long as I could. She warned that if the baby was born too soon, there could be consequences. I had to keep a handle on the stress.

Less than two weeks later, I was right back in the hospital in labor again. This time, the doctors could not stop the contractions easily. They admitted me into the hospital and put me on a medication that had me bedridden for three days. I could not feel my feet under me. I was nauseated and sick. I couldn't do anything for myself. Ethan came to see me the first day that I was admitted and he left me there by myself. I was scared for myself and for the baby. The doctor told me that if I delivered at that time, I would have to leave my baby in the hospital for at least a month, if she survived. She was not ready to be born. I prayed that God would keep her with me and let the contractions stop.

The doctors were able to give me a steroid to help develop her lungs. They wanted me to hold her for two more weeks, and they believed that she would be fine if born at that point.

My mother sent my father home to get some clothes for her. She stayed right by my side the whole time. She even helped me take a bath. She took care of me. I could feel my mother praying for me as I slept. God gave me strength. He answered my mother's prayers. I was dismissed from the hospital. I felt a great deal of peace.

I went back home with Ethan. I was excited that we were about to finally see our baby girl. Her name was all over everything. Ethan began to argue with me about the baby's name. He did not want her name to be Taylor. Everything that made me happy, he was determined to control in some way. He couldn't let me have the joy of picking a name for our daughter. I felt that I deserved that honor. After all, I had been on my own with the help of God and my family for the entire pregnancy.

My little company keeper was on her way, and God knew that I needed her. God reminded me to watch my stress level. I gave in and changed her name to the one that Ethan wanted. I delivered that baby two weeks later, prematurely, at thirty-six weeks. She was a healthy, beautiful baby girl weighing five pounds and eight ounces. When she opened her eyes, they were bright green.

Believe it or not, her eyes matched the name that Ethan picked for her. She was the most beautiful sight that I ever laid eyes on in my life. God brought back to memory the encounter that I had with His messenger six years prior to that day. My baby looked just like the child that the angel described to me. He told me that my firstborn child would be a baby girl. God is awesome, and His power is magnificent.

I was happy. I couldn't believe that I was someone's mother. We spent a couple of days in the hospital, the baby, my mother, and me. Ethan left shortly after the baby was born. All of my family and friends came to see us. I was nervous and afraid that I wasn't going to know how to care for the precious jewel that was given to me from God. I dreaded being dismissed from the hospital. I didn't want to go home. My mother was helping me a great deal. I was still in a lot of pain. I didn't know what I would do without my mother.

The nurse came in and brought my discharge papers. Ethan entered the hospital with all of the children. He brought them to see the baby. He came in the room in a bad mood. I was not in any position to deal with that.

He told his children to get all of my things. He began snatching down the signs that my friends made, welcoming the baby. He handed out gifts and balloons one by one to the children. The nurses were in awe. He didn't speak to anyone. He just began to gather things and ordering the children to take them to the car. He snapped at me because I had on a gown and a housecoat. He said, "I have things to do; you told me you were ready. Why are you not dressed?"

I said, "Ethan, I just had a baby, and I am still in pain. I can't get dressed. This is the outfit I brought to wear home from the hospital."

He said, "You are not going anywhere with me looking like that."

My mother looked at him and said, "You don't have to take her with you; she can go home with me."

He was so shocked that he said, "Fine with me." He left the hospital with the children.

I was relieved. The pain got worse when I arrived to my mother's house. I barely made it to the bed. My mother took care of the baby so that I could rest.

Ethan later called and apologized for the state that he was in when he came to the hospital. He asked if he could come and get the baby and me. He came the next morning. The pain medicine was helping, but it quickly wore off. I couldn't sit long or bend over to change the baby on my own.

My mother called to check on me. She could hear in my voice that I needed her. She came to stay with Ethan, the baby, and me for a week.

I was much better after a few days. I could move around with a little more ease. I truly enjoyed my mother being there to help. My father picked her up at the end of the week. I held back the tears when we stood at the door and waved as they drove away.

After the baby was born, Ethan spent a little more time at home. Any time that he planned a trip away, I planned a trip to go home to visit my family.

I had a lot to look forward to. I was hired as a teacher in the school district where we lived. I was a good teacher. I had a special love for children.

Life at home was very rocky for Ethan and me; sometimes up and sometimes down. There was peace with Ethan's baby's mother, as long as I stayed out of the picture. He did not speak of her unless it was time to keep their daughter. One particular day, he told me that he was going to pick up his child for a weekend visit. I stayed at home while Ethan went to meet her mother to pick her up. I did not complain about it. I made myself a promise that I wasn't going to get upset or bothered. She came to visit. I thought that we had a great weekend. All of a sudden, Ethan decided to call her mother and arrange for her to go home. He came in the bedroom and told me that his baby's mother wanted me to call her. I did not understand why, but I called. She asked me why her daughter had to come home early. I didn't know how to answer the question, because I was as clueless as she was. Apparently he told her that I was sending our child to visit my parents; therefore their child had to go home. I explained to her that Ethan came in and told me that he was sending her home. She told me that Ethan was no good and soon I would see. I proclaimed to her that she should be happy that he was no longer her problem. As she and I talked, we both could clearly see that Ethan was being dishonest with both of us. I felt that she should thank God that she didn't end up with him.

Ethan came in and overheard the conversation. He snatched the phone from me and hung up in her face. He grabbed me and choked me. I felt myself blacking out. As soon as I began to see all black, he released me. As I fell to the floor, he yelled and screamed at me. He eventually went into the guest room and locked the door. I stood outside of the door, and I could hear him trying to explain and console his baby's mother. He was telling her that I was trying to destroy their relationship and come between them. I did not realize that they had a relationship. He always worked hard to convince me that she was crazy, evil, and trying to destroy our relationship.

I was hurt and distraught. I immediately went to our bedroom and packed some clothes. I drove to my parents' house that night. I was very disappointed in him. I did not tell my parents that he put his hands on me. I just explained that we had an argument, and I needed to come home. My parents always opened their doors and their hearts to my child and me.

I looked forward to going to church that Sunday. Church was where I found my strength. As I entered the church, I noticed a new phrase that was posted on the back wall of the church. It said, "Victory is in the Praise." Those words stuck to me like glue. I felt the power of God as I said them to myself. On that day I began to praise God with all my might in a shout and a dance. The more that I shouted, the stronger I felt. During my praise time, I felt very close to God. I was in a place where He could help me. While praising God, I felt free. I forgot that my husband was abusive. I forgot that I had any problems. For that moment, I felt peace. My daughter and I stayed with my parents for a few days. Ethan and I had several conversations during that time. We came to the conclusion that marriage wasn't working for us. He decided to call his attorney to file for a divorce. I was hurt, but I didn't want Ethan to know just how much. He made all of the plans, and I agreed. His attorney prepared all of the paperwork. I did not want my little to girl to grow up in a home without two parents. Ethan proclaimed his love for me, but he acknowledged the fact that he was not making me happy. He asked me to come home and try again. My daughter and I returned home.

When I returned home, things were a little different. Any time that Ethan and I had an argument, he took the keys to the house and to my car. Every time that it happened, it tore me apart. I felt like I did not own anything, and neither did I have a place to call my home, other than the one with my parents. Ethan called his attorney and terminated the divorce decree that had been drawn up. He wasted five hundred dollars.

Ethan took my car for a drive. He returned home in a new car. It was candy apple red. Everyone knows that I dislike the color red. Again, I was grateful because it was another brand-new car. The first car was titled in my name only. The new car was titled in Ethan's name and mine. Ethan and I were working on mending the problems in our relationship.

He didn't keep his youngest daughter much. I loved the little girl. She was a sweet child. The situation with her mother was almost unbearable, though. Ethan was trying to please her mother and me. She was angry when she heard that Ethan bought me a new car. It wasn't long before she had another car also. I enjoyed my car for three months. I got tired of Ethan taking the keys to it every time he got angry at me. I told him that I would purchase a car of my own as soon as I had been on my job a little longer.

Ethan went to the local hardware store and purchased a For Sale sign. He placed it in the window of that car. He began to drive around and advertise the sale of my car. I was hurt. I thought that he would wait until I had enough money for a down payment on one before selling the other one. I prayed that the car would not sell. If it did, I would not have any transportation. Ethan came home and informed me that he found a buyer for the car in a neighboring state. He asked me to drive the car so that he could take it to the buyer. I held back the tears as I signed away the only form of transportation that I had. This event in itself hurt me more than anything that Ethan ever did. I drove Ethan's old truck and did not complain.

One day my father called me to come for a visit. When I arrived, my daddy took me to look at cars. I had just started my job and was beginning to re-establish my credit. I found a car that I really liked. Daddy did all the talking and made a smooth deal. The only problem was that my credit was terrible. The majority of the monthly payment would be going toward interest. I was disappointed, but I knew that I needed a car. Just as I was about to sign on the dotted line, my daddy pulled out his checkbook and paid for the car in full. Daddy told me to pay him when I could. I cried all the way back home. Whenever in need, I knew that I could depend on my parents. I didn't even have to ask.

Ethan felt bad. He later wrote my father a check for the entire amount that he paid for the car. Ethan knew that I had a loving and supportive family who would always be there for me no matter what.

When I heard that Ethan's child's mother had another car, I accused him of being involved with her and getting the car for her. Ethan drew back his fist and hit me as hard as he could. That closed fist landed close to my temple. I saw stars for a while. I learned to use makeup to hide those bruises very well. I told Ethan if he ever hit me again, I would tell my daddy. I meant it with my whole heart, mind, body, and soul. My father told him not to hit me. He told Ethan that if he ever had to do that, to send me back home to him. I was tired of being hit. Ethan knew that I was angry. He knew that as soon as he turned his back I would leave. I wasn't accustomed to being treated that way. He was bigger and taller than me. I knew that I needed to fight back, I didn't know how. I wasn't street wise, so I didn't try to play games with him. I was too scared. The one thing that I had that he couldn't stand was a sharp tongue. When angered, there was no telling what I would say. Ethan frequently told me that I belittled him and made him feel less of a man with my words. When he abused me and disrespected me, it made me angry. When pushed into a corner, anyone would come out fighting. I could not physically beat him in an argument, but I knew that I could always win with words. Ethan would also frequently say, "In any disagreement, it is a battle of who can hurt the other one the worst." Words are all I had. He overshadowed me with everything else.

The following weekend, Ethan mentioned that he was going to pick up the children. He didn't previously let me know that they were coming. I had made plans for the weekend. We had several events going on at the church, and I wanted to be there. I expressed that I couldn't leave and take the baby with me, because the children wanted to spend time with their little sister. Ethan expressed that I wasn't going to leave him stuck at the house with a house full of kids. He got angry and left. I planned on leaving that evening, and Ethan would not allow me to go. When he returned, he didn't have the children with him. I assumed that he decided not to go and get them. He was upset, and he knew that I was upset. We began to argue. He grabbed my face and squeezed my cheeks as hard as he could. I thought that he was going to break my jaw. He continued to hold on. I cried like a baby. I felt his fingernail piercing one side of my face. When he finally let go, I saw blood on one side of my face and a bruise on the other. I tried to get my cell phone. Ethan grabbed it and slammed it into the wall. It shattered into many pieces. Before I knew it, I cursed him out. I ran and grabbed the house phone. Just as promised, I called my daddy. Before Ethan could snatch the phone from me I said, "Daddy, he hit me, and he has been hitting me for a while." Ethan took the phone and hung it up.

My mother called back. Ethan would not allow me to answer. The phone kept ringing. I told Ethan that if he did not allow me to answer, they were going to come over. I answered the phone. I could hear the hurt in my father's voice as he said, "Give Ethan the phone." I don't know what exactly my father said. I watched the expression on Ethan's face. He just sat there and listened.

Before handing me the phone Ethan asked, "Did she tell you that she cursed me out?" He then gave me the phone. I could feel the disappointment in me by my father. My father said, "Tell me you are not over there cursing."

I said, "Daddy, I am so tired."

He said, "You cannot allow the devil to make you get on his level. You have to stay strong." My father then asked, "Are you going to stay with him, or do you want me to come and get you?" I couldn't answer. My daddy explained that if he and my mother got involved in this, they would lose me. He shared that my daughter and I always had a place to come home to, whenever we needed. He told me that he was angry with Ethan. My father knew that if he came over, the situation would be worse. He told me that he would support my decision because he knew that I was in God's hands. I told my dad to give me some time to think about it, and I would call him back.

Ethan apologized and promised that it wouldn't happen again. I apologized for cursing him out. Minutes later I called my father and told him that the baby and I would stay. I also apologized to my parents for letting Ethan get the best of me. I knew that they were disappointed. I usually didn't act like that. It was a long time before Ethan hit me again.

I have an older brother and a younger sister. My parents and I agreed that I should not tell my brother or my sister about Ethan abusing me. My brother would have rallied some allies and staged an attack. People who were dear to me could be hurt. My parents and I kept this secret amongst the three of us.

I had to repent for my actions. I clearly saw that night that there were some things in me that I didn't realize was there. I acknowledged the fact that Ethan wasn't worth missing heaven. I had to be stronger than that in the future.

I was unhappy. The only sense of peace that I had was on Sundays. I drove to my hometown every Sunday for church. I sang in the choir, and I praised God every chance that I got. Ethan did not come to church with me very often. He didn't understand how and why we praise God the way that we do at my church. He would tease me around his family and friends. He imitated the way that I shouted in church. Everyone laughed as if I were a joke. I believed what the sign said on the wall of the sanctuary, "Victory is in the praise." The more that they laughed, the more that I praised Him. God gave me peace in the midst of my storm. My hair even praised God. People would tell me the only thing that they saw when I shouted was my hair. When I finished it fell back in place. Someone once told me that the angels in heaven combed my hair back in place every time that I finished giving God the praise.

My parents had been married more than thirty years. The thought of divorce truly disturbed me. I grew up with both of my parents. I wanted so badly for my daughter to have that as well. I wanted to always be able to tell her that I did everything in my power to make my marriage to her biological father work. Each time that I left and returned it seemed that the amount of hate for me inside of him grew.

I reached out to his children. They each knew how much I loved them. I took a lot of time with them and did everything in my power to give them nice things, just as I did my own daughter. I know that they envied the fact that my daughter was being raised in the house with their daddy, while they were not. I could not change that. I made sure that they felt loved and did not feel that

I was influencing their father to treat them any differently than he did our daughter. When they came over each Christmas, I personally split the money that I saved up to spend on my daughter and made sure that they had a lot of gifts under the tree, just like she did. I tried to have a good relationship with all three of the women that Ethan had children by. I felt that we should get along for the children's sake. As previously stated, one of them would never give me a chance. She felt that I took something from her. But at this point, I hope that she realizes that my coming into Ethan's life was not a curse for her, but a blessing.

I had a feeling that Ethan was being unfaithful to me. I did not have any proof. At one point I felt that Ethan was cheating on me with his son's mother. All of a sudden he began picking up his child by her and her other children from school. I did not trust Ethan as far as I could throw him. I did not know her. Ethan never did anything unless there was something involved that benefitted him. I questioned him about it. As usual, we argued. Instead of Ethan trying to include me in decisions and talking to me about this, he called his son's mother and told her that I had a problem with her other children being at our house and riding home from school with him. She and I were cordial to each other prior to that, and we made every effort to get along. All of the progress that we exerted to build a friendship for the children's sake was almost destroyed. I soon learned this was how Ethan liked things. He loved controversy and confusion, especially with the women in his life. His oldest children's mother never fell for those kinds of games. She and I always got along. I'm sure that Ethan tried to turn her against me also. She never gave me any inclination that she felt any ill will toward me. Many Sundays she and the kids went to church with me. We took the children to the county fair together on occasion. We had a good relationship. Over time Ethan's son's mother saw that I loved her child. I believe that she looked past the bad picture that Ethan portrayed to her about me. We never experienced anything negative after that point. We built a friendship for her son because it was in his best interest.

I tried to ignore the feelings that I had about Ethan and his youngest child's mother. It was hard. I knew that there was another woman who shared a bond with my husband that I just could not understand.

Ethan had many brothers and sisters. One of them had a hard time, and she needed some help. She was about twenty years old. She was pregnant, and she and her boyfriend were having problems. She asked Ethan if she could move in with us for a while. It was nice to have her there at first. After a while strange things began to happen. One particular day, I came home from work and she was sitting in Ethan's favorite chair with him. I got a sick feeling in the pit of my stomach. I went to the refrigerator and fixed me something to drink. When I turned around, she had moved to the couch. I never said a word about it. Later that week, she told me that she had something to talk to me about that disturbed her. She told me that Ethan made a pass at her. I did not trust Ethan, but it sounded outrageous, even for him. I did not tell him for a day or so. I prayed and contemplated how to handle it. I questioned her a little more, because it seemed so unbelievable. I organized the facts. He is her stepbrother. They met a few months prior to this occurrence. They did not grow up together. They were related by blood, but they did not have a sisterly and brotherly bond. She said that Ethan asked her if he could give her a massage while she was lying on the bed. He went under her shirt and touched her in ways a man would who was not related to her. Ethan denied all of this. He got angry with her and told her that she had to leave.

I was puzzled, because it seemed that so many women that came into his life always lied about him. That was his story. I believed the old saying, "If a lot of people are saying smoke, there is a fire near." After she packed her things and left, I questioned him more. My instincts told me that Ethan was not completely innocent. He got angry at me and grabbed a small bag to leave for the night. I told him that I could not take anymore. I tossed my wedding ring at him, and it landed somewhere in the front yard. He picked it up and got in his truck and left. He returned a little after 4:00 in the morning. He told me the next morning that he drove to the next state and drove around to think. He worked hard to convince me that we could get past his sister's lies.

I was so miserable that I needed some help. I knew what to do in time of despair. I knew to call on Jesus. The church was having a revival on Friday night. If I could make it to that point, I would be all right. I was drained, physically and mentally. I had a feeling that something was about to unfold. I did not know what. I felt compelled to go to the revival. As I headed out of town to my church, a car was tailing me very closely. I didn't think anything strange about it. I kept driving. The car pulled up beside me and let the window down. The young woman who was driving motioned for me to let down my window. When I did, she asked, "Do you know who I am?"

I looked at her very closely, and I knew. She was Ethan's youngest child's mother. His daughter looked just like her. It had been years since I had seen her. I really did not remember what she looked like. She tried to get me to pull the car over. I refused. I always followed my instincts and the voice of God. I heard God say, "No." She got angry that I would not pull over.

She yelled, "When your husband came home at 4:00 in the morning the other day, he had been with me." I felt like someone took a knife and stuck it right through my heart. I called him and asked two questions that list as follows: "Why do you keep betraying me with this woman? What does she have on you?"

He tried to explain.

I told him good-bye and I hung up the phone. My phone rang for the entire time that I drove to church. My goal was to get to revival, and I knew that God would do the rest. The state that I was in, I could not go any further, and I knew it. I sat in church and went through the motions. That night I was too broken, busted, and discouraged to even shout. All kinds of thoughts were going through my mind. The only reason for me to continue with life was my child. I felt that she needed me, and I knew I could not leave her with him. As I wallowed in self-pity, the guest speaker called me to the altar. She laid her hand on my forehead and began to pray for me. It felt like virtue left her body and transformed into strength for me. The more that she prayed, the stronger I felt. God began to speak through her as she spoke in tongues. I felt the power of God strongly in that building. I will never forget what she said to me. She hugged me and said, "God says you can make it. Don't give up. Just hold on a little while longer, just a little while longer."

I cried out to God. When I left that altar, I was free. I stayed the night at my parents' house. I slept very well. I knew that God was with me. The only option that I had was to trust Him. I knew that it wasn't over. I knew that all of my questions were about to be answered. I had a strong feeling. The next day, I went back home.

Ethan did not know how to read me. I was at peace. I was hurt and angry with him, but I felt God with me. I looked forward to the time for me to go to work. That time took my mind off my problems at home. As the students filled the classroom, I went to sit at my desk. One of my classroom assistants took attendance, and the other one went to check the faculty box for our classroom. When she returned she placed all the contents on my desk. When I flipped through, I found a white envelope addressed to me. It did not have a return address. I heard a still voice say, "Throw it away." Out of curiosity, I did not. I opened it and read. It was nine pages long, front and back. It did not take me long to realize that the letter was from Ethan's youngest child's mother. She informed me that she and Ethan had been involved the whole time that we were married. She knew that Ethan had filed for divorce. She knew every detail that took place in our marriage. She listed them in chronological order in the letter. She knew things about my family, personal things. She described the inside of my home. She wrote that her goal was to destroy our marriage, and that Ethan was stupid to trust her. I will never forget the last statement in the letter. It read something to the extent that, "The man that you sleep next to every night is your worst enemy." When I finished reading the letter, I tried to stand up beside my desk. I was so taken by surprise that I almost passed out. I could hear one of the women in the room praying, "Lord whatever it is, give her strength." She began the lesson, and the other assistant walked me outside. She told me to get some air, and I would feel better. I told my assistants that I was feeling sick. I was too embarrassed to show them the letter.

I called Ethan and asked him to come to my job. When he arrived, I could not say a word. I just handed the letter to him. He read the first couple of pages and gave it back to me. I went back into my classroom and finished the day with my kids. They gave me life. I left the letter with Ethan. Words cannot describe how betrayed I felt. I had answers. Now I knew what she was using to blackmail Ethan. I wanted to leave. There was no trust. We did not have anything left to build our marriage on.

I went to my parents' home as soon as Ethan left for work. I did not take any clothing with me. My baby did not have diapers or milk, and my funds were very low. I was upset when I left the house. I got in the car and drove. I went into my parents' house, and my family could instantly tell that something was very wrong.

After talking for a while, I stated that I needed some extra clothes and the baby needed her things. I knew that Ethan was at work and he would not be home until the next day. My sister and I drove back to my home to get some things. While packing, I heard Ethan pull up in the front yard. He was outraged that I was packing some of our things. I needed some time away from him. I needed to sort through this newfound information. Ethan was so angry that he began to throw our things into the front yard. He threw the baby's walker and high chair out there also. I did not have enough room in the car to take all that stuff with me. I had come only for a few clothes and baby items.

He went into my closet and threw large piles of my clothing in the yard. While he was tossing some of the household items outside, he dropped a vase and broke it in the foyer. As he threw out more of the baby's things, I begged him to stop. He grabbed me by my hair and pulled me toward the door.

He pulled me so hard that my flip-flops came off my feet. My feet began to bleed as he pulled me through the glass. It hurt so bad that I screamed.

My sister was in the other room. When she heard my screams, she ran into the room with us. When she entered, she had a butcher knife in her hand. I was proud of her that day. I didn't realize until then that even though she is the baby of the family, she is the strongest one of us.

She looked Ethan in his eyes and said, "If you don't get your hands off my sister, I will kill you." Ethan immediately let me go. He told us to get out of his house. He locked the doors and left us standing in the front yard. I will never forget that scene. It was unreal. It looked like something that you would see on television. Many of our things were scattered all over the front yard. I was glad that I had left the baby with my mother.

The police were called. They arrived as Ethan was getting in his truck to go back to work. They told me that since we were married, they could not get involved. They told me that I could come to the station and sign an order so that the judge would grant me permission to come back into the house to get the rest of my things. I stood there and cried, because I did not know what I would do with all my things that were lying in the yard.

My sister consoled me and told me that everything would be okay. Some of the neighbors came outside and asked if we needed anything. We fit everything that we could into the car. A lot of our belongings were still lying in the yard. As we stood there looking, one of the neighbors offered to put the rest in an empty room in her house. I thanked her, and I thanked God for her. She was very helpful. She told me that my stuff could stay in her home as long as needed.

My sister and I went back to my parents' home. My sister was furious with Ethan. I felt that she would never forgive him for what she saw that day.

Ethan later called and said he was filing for a divorce. I didn't know how to feel, because the pain was so intense. I loved Ethan regardless of how he hurt me.

I lived with my parents for approximately three weeks as Ethan and I prepared to go through a divorce. I couldn't hide from my family how hurt I was. I didn't want them to know that deep down, I missed Ethan and that I wanted to go home. I was ashamed, because the man treated me so badly. How could I get anyone to understand why I still loved him?

I returned to our home to sign the divorce papers. When I got ready to sign, I began to cry. Ethan asked me if this was what I really wanted. I told him that I didn't know what I wanted. He suggested that we try one more time. He told me that his child's mother no longer had anything to hold over our heads. He assured me that we could be happy now, and things would be the way that they were meant to be. I gave Ethan another chance, and I went back home to be with him.

I could tell that my sister was angry with me. It was a long time before she would be in the same room with Ethan. I knew that she highly disliked him.

I was determined to make my marriage work. I felt that I owed it to my daughter. We built a life and a home for her. I should try.

Ethan was very controlling and untrusting of me. He always treated me as though I was going to cheat on him. He wouldn't let me go to the grocery store by myself. I did not have any friends. He did not want me close to anyone but him. One particular day Ethan was about to go to work. I previously expressed to him that I wanted to go to my hometown to go to choir rehearsal. He did not want me to go. He took the keys to my car, the house keys, and my cell phone. I followed him out to his truck as he was about to leave for work. I asked him to please give me back my things and not to leave me at the house overnight without transportation or a phone. He ignored me and got into his truck. I had an umbrella in my hand. I was so angry with him that I threw the umbrella at his truck. He got out of his truck and walked into the garage. He picked up a sledgehammer and broke every window in my car with the exception of the back window. He left the hammer lodged in the last window that he broke. He cut his hand as glass shattered from the broken windows. Blood was everywhere. Ethan went into the house to wash his hands. For the first time, I fought back. I grabbed the hammer and cracked his front windshield. He then got in his truck and left for work. I went and got my camera and took pictures of my car. I still have those pictures in my possession. I called my father and told him what happened.

When my parents arrived, my mother helped me clean up the blood. I took my father to the garage and showed him my car. He stood there and shook his head. He could not believe it.

I got some of the baby's things and what I needed for a few days. We left with my parents. When I returned home a few days later, all the windows on my car were replaced and re-tinted.

I frequently thought of the line that Ethan's baby's mother put in her letter to me. She said that the man that I slept next to every night was my worst enemy. Ethan had serious problems controlling his temper.

My memories and feelings were really starting to get to me. I read that letter from Ethan's baby's mother over and over again. Ethan and I discussed or argued about the contents of it every other day. God spoke to me one day and told me to destroy the letter. I obeyed and threw it in the fireplace. Once that happened, our arguments about it slowly decreased. I started working toward putting that hurt behind me. The problem with putting hurt behind me was that Ethan continued to do things to hurt me. I felt that he was constantly throwing salt on an open wound.

I felt alone in that town. I had few people I could trust or talk to. I felt comfortable talking to my daddy, though. God began to deal with me about my father. My daddy did not say too much at all when I talked to him about every episode that Ethan and I experienced. Talking to my father was an outlet for me. I did not have to hold in all of my pain. I could trust him. He listened to me. He gave me an opportunity to get a lot off my chest. He did not judge or criticize. He didn't seem to hold any grudges against anyone. He would always put people in God's hands. I watched my father age before my eyes. His hair was almost completely gray. He also frequently suffered with different ailments. He and my mother started a very healthy diet. As I prayed for him, God showed me that I was draining him. He couldn't take watching me hurt so badly, and there was nothing that he could do to ease my pain. My heart was broken. Every conversation that I had with my daddy was little by little breaking his heart. I am his daughter; he was hurting right along with me. The hurt was starting to have a negative effect on his health.

When God allowed me to see myself, I knew that I was about to lose my closest confidant. I could not hurt my daddy any more. I had to stop talking to him so much about my problems. I didn't know what I was going to do. Not only did I need my father's listening ear, I needed his spiritual advice. God assured me that He would send me a friend I could trust and confide in.

I was on my way to church one Sunday. Ethan's three girls spent the weekend with us. Since they lived so close to my church, I gave them a ride home. My phone rang as soon as I was an hour away from home. The caller ID displayed the number to be unavailable. Every time I answered, the person did not say anything. I dropped off the girls and went to church. I received the same call all through church. I did not answer. As soon as I got in my car to proceed home, the phone rang again. This time I answered. I could hear the person breathing. I said, "You seem to want to talk to me; please say something."

The person said, "Someone wants you to have some information. They really think a lot of you. They asked me to call." It was a man's voice on the other end of the phone. He told me that he did not know me. He kept assuring me that someone asked him to call. He told me to brace myself. He explained that what he was about to tell me would really hurt. He told me as soon as I pulled out of the driveway with Ethan's children in the car earlier that Sunday morning, a woman pulled up. He described the young woman, told me where she worked, and described her car. He also told me that a young woman who drives a black pickup truck came in and out of my home like she was a key-holding resident. She came during the week around the same time on the days that Ethan was off work. Ethan pulled his truck up on the side of our home, and she pulled up beside him. I was told that some days Ethan took our daughter into the house and then he came back to the door to escort in the young woman. I knew the identity of the mystery woman described by the stranger on the other end of my phone. She was Ethan's ex-girlfriend from years past. I remember coming home from work at lunchtime one day. I went in the restroom to comb my hair. I saw long strings of reddish-blond hair in the bathroom sink. When I questioned Ethan, he explained that it was his daughter's hair. She had long braids. As usual, I believed him. His ex-girl friend had long reddish-blond hair. I did not make the connection until I listened to the stranger on the other end of the phone. I questioned him more about the young woman who was in my home on this day. He told me that the person who gave him the information would talk to me, if I could be trusted. I explained that I did not trust anyone. He said, "I am going to have the person call you."

A few minutes later, I received a call from an individual. I had a lot of questions. This person mainly wanted assurance I could be trusted. I gave my word that I would never share their identity with Ethan.

Our home was like open season. Ethan allowed any women he desired to come there when I wasn't home. For some reason, I could never get comfortable in that house. I did not feel that it was my home. After my conversation with the individual I knew why. I wasn't the only queen of that home. I was told that I was such a good person and I deserved so much better than the treatment and disrespect that I received from Ethan. When I arrived at my so-called home, I greeted Ethan and looked around. I looked to see if any pictures had been moved or if I could detect any trace of this woman. He asked me what was wrong. He was dressed and prepared to go to work. I waited until he got to work, and I was on my way to a hotel in town, before I told him about my phone call. He denied everything for six whole hours. Finally there was a knock at the hotel door. It was Ethan. He found me. I told him that he could not enter until he was ready to tell me the truth. He admitted to me that the young woman had been in our home with him that day. He came up with some story about the fact that he was doing some work on her car.

Ethan was being watched, and he did not know it. The reporter of his wrongdoings told me the time that she arrived and the time that she left. There was no work being done on any car, not that day. I was growing very tired of Ethan and his issues with women. No matter what I did, I was not enough for him. He had to be entangled with two or three women at a time.

I needed proof, though. All I got from him was a lot of lies. I drove by the movie rental store the next day until I saw the car that was described to me. When I knew she was there, I walked in. I walked up to the front counter and asked to see her. The other young woman stood there with her mouth open as soon as she saw me. Even she knew the girl had been having dealings with my husband. I asked, "Why were you at my home yesterday?"

She said, "Please, let's go outside and talk about this." When we got outside, she explained that he told her I wouldn't have a problem with it. I told her that I knew she was married. I asked her if she would like another woman being in her home. She quickly said, "No." She explained that she only came by to pick up a movie that she let him borrow. I began to drown her out. I don't remember what else she said. I left the store and went home.

I was tired, sick and tired of Ethan. As usual, he promised to make up for this. I knew that there was nothing that he could do to make me trust him again, nothing. I didn't have anyone to talk to. I had just promised God that I would lay off of my daddy.

I started having anxiety attacks. During those attacks, my heart would beat very fast and I would get a shortness of breath. I went to see a new doctor in town. He asked me if I was stressed out at home or at work. I acted as if I had no idea what he was speaking about. He gave me a prescription that would take the edge off and make me feel better. He told me that it was only a temporary fix. He suggested that I figure out what the problem was and get rid of it. I took the pills for two days and discontinued use of them. Those pills made me feel funny, like I was floating on a cloud. My job required me to be alert. I could not function on my job feeling that way.

I worked as a teacher. I was doing very well. My supervisor encouraged me to go back to school and get my certification to be an administrator. Enrolling in school was a good move for me. I really needed something to take my focus off my situation at home. While in school I obtained two additional degrees while continuing to work as a teacher. I also maintained a 4.0 grade average while getting those degrees. When I completed my certification in administration, I was promoted to assistant principal. This promotion required me to move to another school. Before I left my current school, God blessed me to make friends with a very special woman. Many Tuesdays she rode with me to my former town to go to choir rehearsal. I did not want to get too far behind on the songs for the choir. She kept my little one and me company while we faithfully took that drive.

Starting my new position as assistant principal was another struggle. Many people did not feel that I deserved the promotion. I had taught only three years in that school district, and I moved right into administration. I honestly felt that my new supervisor had someone else in mind to be her assistant. I was placed there against her wishes. I encountered a lot of stress and opposition because of that placement. Even in the midst of that, God was with me. I was really having a hard time dealing with the pressure. This new position entailed more time away from home, and I made more money, which in itself was intimidating to Ethan. He consistently accused me of thinking that I was much better than him because I made more money and I had more degrees than he did.

I was trying very hard to hold it together. I was under pressure at home and at work. I didn't feel wanted or appreciated in either place.

God honored His promise to me. I was sitting in choir rehearsal one evening when a woman came to me and told me that God placed me on her heart. She wanted her niece and me to become friends. She said that we had a lot in common. She suggested that I call her. Usually I wouldn't agree to anything like that, but I felt led to do it. I called the woman's niece. She and I talked for hours that one night. We have been talking every since. Since I gave God my word that I would ease up on my daddy's ears, He sent me a friend. She is one of my best friends to this day. I call her My Sister in Christ.

I started having anxiety attacks again. I was on my way to choir rehearsal. My friend did not come with me for this trip. I had been on the road for ten minutes, and I began to hyperventilate. I could not catch my breath. I was sweating, and my heart was racing. I stopped the car and put it in park. I began to cry. My daughter started crying also. I remember her saying, "Mama, what is wrong." I grabbed my cell phone, and I called my daddy. As soon as he answered, I told him that I was scared. I could not tell my father where I was. I didn't know myself. He could hear my daughter crying too. My daddy prayed for me and prayed to bind the devil. After a little while, I calmed down, and I was able to recognize my surroundings. Episodes such as that one became more frequent.

I was sitting at my desk at work, and the secretary transferred a call to me. It was a young woman that Ethan had previously had dealings with. She shared with me that Ethan had been trying to pursue her. Her fiancé found out about it and confronted Ethan. He and Ethan apparently had a serious altercation. I asked, "How can I help you? What is your purpose for calling me?" She told me that she wanted me to have Ethan to leave her alone; he was causing problems in her relationship.

I returned to work right away, but when I got home, I asked Ethan about the things that the young woman told me. He denied all of it, swearing that she was interested in him. I did a little research of my own. I called the fiancé myself. I must admit he was a gentleman about the whole situation. He told me that it wasn't his place to tell me what Ethan was up to. He said that Ethan should do it himself. I told him that I respected that.

In a later discussion with Ethan, I mentioned the fact that I called that guy. Ethan was so furious with me that he rolled up a newspaper and slapped me across the face with it. He pushed me to the ground and held my face to the floor with the bottom of his dirty shoe. When he finally released me, I looked in the mirror. I could see the print mark from the bottom of Ethan's shoe on my cheek. I cried myself to sleep that night. I was very tired.

I soon broke out in hives that would last twenty minutes or so. Once I calmed down, they would disappear. I went to see an allergist, trying to get a handle on the cause of the hives, which were quite bothersome. I felt like I was losing my mind.

One evening we were watching a movie as a family. I began to itch and scratch uncontrollably. I had huge welts all over my body wherever I scratched. My daughter was normal and so was he. I convinced myself that he must have something to do with what was happening to me. I stopped eating any food that Ethan prepared or brought to me. I refused to let him bring me lunch. I did not trust Ethan, nor did I understand what was happening. I was sitting at my desk one day, and I could feel hives forming on my face. I was tired and irritated by this. I asked for permission to go to the doctor. I walked in to see the doctor that diagnosed my first anxiety attack. He looked at me and said, "I remember you. You still haven't figured out the problem, huh?" I described to him what I had been going through. He told me that it was stress. He told me that I was very sick. He said the sickness was housed in my mind. He wrote me a two-month prescription that would help me to get a hold of my life and get it together. He told me that the pills he prescribed were highly addictive. He told me that those pills would only be a Band-aid for me. They would not fix my problem. He told me that two months' worth of pills was all he could give me. He told me not to come back for more, because he would not give me another prescription. His last words to me were, "Take this time, figure out what the problem is, and get rid of it."

I cried all the way back to work. I asked, "God, how am I supposed to get rid of my husband? He is driving me crazy." I literally meant that, crazy. I got on the computer and did a little research on the pill that had been prescribed to me. It was a nerve pill. My state of mind was in serious jeopardy. I no longer had an outlet. All of the drama, my issues with Ethan, and my thoughts had made me sick. I decided to go ahead and take that medicine. I needed help. I could not function the way that I was going. Two days after I started taking the medicine, the hives stopped. I slept like a baby at night. I was relaxed. I felt in control of my life. As far as I was concerned things were good, until I began to think about death. I thought about dying quite frequently. Out of nowhere, the thoughts would come. Other than that, I felt that I had it together. I never told Ethan or my parents that I was taking this prescription.

When I was a couple of weeks away from finishing my two-month supply, Ethan came in and started in on me about working late. I lost it. I threw the pill bottle on the bed and told him that I needed him to lay off. I said, "I have fourteen pills left. When they are gone, I won't be able to function. Please give me a break."

He was hurt to see me like that. He was also disappointed that I was so dependent on this medicine. He promised to ease up and help me out more.

I was two pills away from an empty bottle, and I was terrified. I did not want to go back to the state that I was in before I started the medicine. I called my mother and told her that I thought I was addicted to pills for nerves and depression. She was hurt. She talked for a minute and told me that she would call me back. Minutes later my daddy called me. He asked me what led me to go and get them. I filled in all of the blanks. I reminded my father of the night that he prayed for me, when I forgot where I was. I told him I had many more episodes like that afterwards. I told him about the hives and that I just couldn't take it anymore. I needed some help. I didn't know what to do.

He told me in a calm voice that everything would be okay. Daddy always made me feel better. A week after I finished that prescription, the hives returned, and they were worse than before. The episodes lasted longer, and my skin felt like it was on fire. I couldn't take it. It was unbearable. I started taking allergy pills, which relieved the hives.

One particular day someone gave me some allergy pills that lasted twenty-four hours. I ran into the house and threw them on the bed. I called for Ethan. I said, "Look what I got!" I realized that I had a serious problem.

My father called to check on me. He always knew when I needed him. He asked how I was doing with the pill situation. I told him that I finished those pills, but I had begun to take some allergy pills that temporarily relieved the hives. My daddy told me to quit taking all of it cold turkey.

I said, "Daddy, I can't. I need it. I can't stand the way the hives feel. They will come back if I stop."

My daddy said, "I am praying for you. God will help you to beat this." Before he hung up, he said, "You have to stop."

J. JACKSON

THE DAY THAT I BEGAN TO LIVE

I went to work like any other day. We were preparing for the state standardized tests. A guest motivational speaker came to speak to our students about the importance of doing their best on tests. As my supervisor prepared for the pep rally, she asked me to take the speaker's wife to pick up lunch for the two of them. Ethan had been calling all morning. I kept telling him that it was a busy day and we had a lot going on. I did not get a chance to call and tell him that I was leaving the school.

As I was driving down the street, I passed Ethan. He called my cell phone. I did not want to answer, because I knew that he would be yelling and cursing at me, and I did not want the woman in the car with me to pick up on the fact that something was wrong. I arrived back to the school to drop the motivational speaker's wife off at the front door. As she got out of the car, my phone rang. It was Ethan. I told the speaker's wife that I would be right back. As I expected, he yelled and screamed and cursed. He did not give me a chance to explain. I told him to meet me at the house.

As I was riding down the street, Ethan pulled up behind me. He tailed me as closely as he could. As I pulled in the driveway, he was so close on me that I thought that he was going to run into the back of my car. I prayed that he did not hurt me. I knew that I had to go back to work. I was not in the mood for hiding any more bruises. I heard God say, "Don't argue with him; stay calm."

I went into the house. Ethan was yelling and screaming accusations at me about cheating on him. He accused me of avoiding him all day and leaving school to meet up with other guys. I tried to explain that I was taking the motivational speaker's wife to get lunch. He would not listen to me. He kept accusing me and yelling at me. I fell on the floor, and I began to cry. I cried hard and so long as I lay on the kitchen floor. Lying there in my own tears, I heard God say, "Have you had enough yet?"

I looked up to heaven. I said, "God, I am so tired. I just can't take anymore."

God spoke again. "I never told you to take any of this. I never told you to get in this situation. If you let me, I will help you."

Ethan tried to help me up. My face and my hair was soaking wet from my tears. He apologized to me. It didn't change the pain I felt. My heart ached so much that I was numb. I went back to work and finished out the day.

I was very excited because my four-year-old daughter was having a preschool prom. She was excited, too. I dressed her in a beautiful velvet and satin dress. I never saw her look as beautiful as she did that day. I put on my best red suit to escort her. As we were preparing to leave the house, Ethan said that we were not going. I begged him not to ruin the day for our daughter. She was very excited and looking forward to it. Ethan poured a cup of beer and placed a top on it so no one would know what he was drinking. He got in the car with us to go to the school. When we walked in, all the students were seated up front. My daughter went to join her friends. I sat back and smiled as she walked away. Many parents were talking to me and complimenting my daughter and me. They knew me from my school.

Ethan sat in the back, off to himself, sipping on the disguised cup of beer, which was unlike him. He never drank like that in public. After being there thirty minutes, Ethan told me that he was ready to leave. I asked him not to make our daughter leave. She was having such a good time. She was running around in the middle of the floor with the other little children chasing balloons. I walked over to her and told her that we had to go. She began to cry. She cried frantically all the way to the car. I cried along with her, until we made it to our home. I was very angry with Ethan. I told him that I was tired of living, and especially being with him.

He said, "I am sick of hearing you talk about dying. You want to die? Wait just a minute." He grabbed our little girl and slung her onto the bed in her room. I was standing behind him crying and screaming that he had to stop being so rough with her. He told her not to get out of her bed and to stay in her room. She cried and screamed at the top of her lungs. He grabbed me and pulled me by my arm into our bedroom. When we got there, I told him that I was tired of all the pressure that he put on me. I yelled, screamed, and cried about how displeased I was with all of the events that took place that day. I told him that I had to take the hurt that he inflicted on me, but now he hurt our daughter. I could still hear her crying in her room. I told Ethan that I'd rather die than continue living the way that I was.

He said, "I'm tired of you saying that." He left the room.

As he walked back toward the bedroom, I heard my daughter say, "Daddy, no! What are you going to do with that?" She cried louder and harder than before. I knew he had a gun. I could feel it. He told my daughter to get back in her room and not to come out. He walked into our room and slammed the gun on top of my tall jewelry box. The gun was loaded and pointed at me. He said, "What happed to all that talking you were doing? Say something now!"

I was so terrified. I did not know what was about to happen to me. I had already said several times that same day that I wanted to die. I talked to God. I said, "Not like this. I did not mean it. God, please help me. I want to live." Everything was happening fast. I could hear my little girl outside the door yelling and crying for me. I saw different scenes from my life flash before me. I saw myself sitting in my kindergarten classroom. I saw the day my friends and I sang to each other in eighth grade, saying good-bye. I saw myself dressed in white at my high school graduation. I saw my daughter being placed in my arms for the first time.

Our daughter was banging on our bedroom door for dear life. Ethan was so angry that it was as if I weren't looking at him, when I looked in his eyes. He was someone else. I was looking into the eyes of something evil. I heard God say, "Stay calm. Don't say a word. Keep eye contact with him, and don't let him see that you are afraid." I obeyed the voice of God. I did not part my mouth.

Ethan kept taunting me, saying, "Say something now, you big and bad."

I kept quiet and never stopped looking him in the eyes. I told God quietly, "If you let me live, I will get my daughter, and we will get out of here." I knew God was with me.

Soon Ethan came to himself, and he apologized. He let me out of the room, and he went and put away the gun.

I grabbed my baby and hugged her as hard as I could, because I thought I was about to die. I thought I would never hold her again. I told her that everything would be okay. She sat on the couch, and I headed to my room to lie down. As I walked away, I heard Ethan tell her not to tell anyone about what happened that day. He was giving her a speech about keeping what happens in the house between us.

I said, "No, if you don't want her to repeat things, then you shouldn't do them." I told my little girl to tell whomever she wanted.

We went to the grocery store later on. As soon as we entered, I took my daughter to pick something that she wanted. It was a routine that I bought her a toy on bad family days. She was used to it.

The next morning my mother drove halfway to meet me to pick up my daughter. She kept her for me on days that I had school. I drove back home, and I went to my Saturday class as planned. I was halfway through my class when my phone rang. It was my mother. She called several times. I left class to return her call. When I answered, she said, "Please tell me that what this child is telling me is not the truth." I told my mother that everything that my daughter said was the truth. I could feel the tears in my mother's eyes. She said, "How can I rest, and you are there alone?" I asked my mother to trust me as I trust God. I assured my mother that I was in God's hands.

The very next day Ethan got dressed for work, preparing to work a twenty-four-hour shift. I hugged him good-bye. For some reason, I felt that this good-bye was permanent. From the front window of the house I watched him drive away. When I could no longer see his truck, I ran and quickly grabbed everything that would fit and packed it in my car. I felt a great deal of relief as I headed for my father's house. I looked in the mirror that morning and I said to myself, "You are so much more than what you have become."

Like the prodigal son, I went home. During my drive home, I felt peace. I knew that my decision was the best one for my daughter and me.

My family was at church. When they got home, I was there putting away my things. My father looked at me, and he smiled. He had a look of peace all over him. He and my mother assured me that they would help my daughter and me with whatever we needed. Daddy said, "As long as you need, our house is your house. You are home." They gave my daughter and me our own rooms, right next to each other. My mother told me to rest, and we would talk the next day. I took her advice. I went to sleep. I was at peace in my home.

The next day, my father told me that we should talk. He sat on the staircase, and I stood and listened. When Daddy summoned anyone for a talk, it was serious. He asked, are you still having hives? I dropped my head as I told my father that I was still taking allergy pills. He told me again, "You have to stop. Just quit; you can do it." He told me that the hives would probably come back. He said they would more than likely burn. Like any fire, they would burn out. He told me that all of the medicines that I had been taking were fueling the fire. He encouraged me to stop and let the hives burn out. He told me that he and my mother would help me to get through the situation. He took his blessed oil and anointed me. He and my mother surrounded me and prayed for me. I felt the power of God so strong in that room. My daddy asked me to give him my word that I would stop. He said, "I can't do it for you. You have to do it on your own." I gave my daddy my word.

I looked in my drawer and got out all of those pills. I threw them in the trash. Twenty-four hours later, the hives returned. My skin was on fire. I walked into my father's room and lay on the bed. I cried as I showed him my skin. It was red, itching, and burning. He said, "If you stick it out, the hives will burn out." For three whole days the burning and itching was unbearable. On the third day, the hives were still there, but not as bad. My mother came into my room to check on me before she and my father went to church. I told her that I couldn't move. I was so weak that I couldn't get out of bed. She called for my daddy. I heard her tell him that she sensed an evil presence in that room. I'd never heard my mother pray like that before. She told the devil, "Take your hands off our child. You have no room here. You cannot have her mind. Let her go now!" I did not have the strength to open my mouth and pray. As she and my father continued to pray, I began to receive some strength. My mother told me to get up out of the bed. I got up, and she helped me get ready for church. I had to lead a song that Sunday in the choir. It was the dedication Sunday for our new sanctuary. As I sang, I was still faintly itching, but I could feel God healing me. I claimed my healing that day. Daddy was right, every day got better. The hives returned occasionally, but they were tolerable. Eventually they burned out. From the first day that they began, the hives lasted a total of seven months.

Ethan called daily. He was apologetic for his actions. I couldn't trust that he had my safety and the safety of my daughter at heart. I couldn't ignore the fact that we were days from being at gunpoint. Ethan came to visit us several times. Many times we went out to the movies and out to dinner. We spent a lot of time talking. Ethan wanted my daughter and me to come home. I was truly afraid of his actions when he got angry. Ethan began to show up at church services. He came some Wednesday nights and Sunday nights. That was what I had been praying for since the day we got married, but it did not feel right. I could not shake the bad feeling that I had about it. Every time that Ethan randomly showed up at church, I had no emotions. I did not feel anything. My heart was cold for him. He walked into church one Sunday morning and sat on the front row. I just looked at him. When the pastor made the appeal for salvation, Ethan went to the altar and said that he wanted to be saved. All of a sudden, it finally hit me. "This must be real," I thought. This man is truly standing here before God with a sorrowful heart, ready to give his life to the God. Like any other saved praying wife that has an unsaved husband, I threw my hands up and cried out as I thanked God. I looked at Ethan, and tears began to fall from his eyes as my father prayed the prayer of repentance with him. I knew that God was going to tell me something. As I went to my seat, I patiently waited to hear His voice. I distinctly heard God say, "Don't you make a move until you see me. If I am a part of this, you will eventually see me. Continue to watch him."

After church, everyone came to me and gave me many hugs as they proclaimed their happiness for Ethan and me. It didn't feel like I always imagined it would feel, the day that Ethan got saved. People shook his hand and gave him the right hand of fellowship. One person walked to my car with me and said, "I know what you saw here today; God told me to tell you to do what He told you to do." I knew that I had to obey God and continue to watch.

Ethan continued to visit, and he continued to try to talk me into returning home. My parents were getting ready to go on a church trip. I told myself that if I was going to return home with Ethan, I should do it while my parents were gone; therefore the transition would be easier for all involved.

Before I had gone home to my parents' house, my credit had become excellent. The last two cars that Ethan and I purchased were in my name. He especially loved the last one. It was the car he always dreamed of driving. During the time that I stayed with my parents, we alternated driving this car. While my parents were away, God spoke to me and told me to get rid of that car. I called my father and told him what God said. My father advised me to obey God and check into it. I took the car to the original dealer and talked to the manager. I explained my situation and told him that I really needed to get out of that car. He made me an offer for it on the spot. That offer entailed my being upside down five thousand dollars. The manager made the offer good for thirty days. He told me to take a few days to think about it and make sure that it was what I wanted.

Ethan kept the car the last week that it was in my name. I eventually broke the news to him that I was coming to get it to sell it. I knew that God controlled the situation. Ethan did not get angry. He gracefully turned the car over to me. I could see that it hurt. I immediately went to the dealership and sold the car to the manager. I also cut him a check for five thousand dollars.

Two days later, I had a dream. I dreamed that a woman was moving into my house with Ethan. I dreamed that she was unpacking food and all of her belongings as if her move there were permanent. The dream was so real to me that I called while I was on my way to church and shared it with Ethan. He went off on me. He called me every name but a child of God. After that, he hung up the phone in my face. The next time that we talked, he shared with me that he had met someone. As he described the young woman, he said that she reminded him so much of me. He then stated that God sent her to him. I laughed until I could not laugh anymore, because I knew that God was not going to send a married man a new woman. I couldn't see that. I called all my friends and told them. We all laughed about it.

Ethan and the young woman got closer and closer. I even found out that she met his ex-wife to pick up his little girls. I began to wonder if the young woman had been a part of Ethan's life longer than he was letting on. There was no way that he would allow a perfect stranger to drive across two states with his children. He trusted the woman, and I could see that.

Ethan asked to keep our daughter, and when she came home, she shared with me that the woman and her child spent the night there in our house with them. Many people were calling me and telling me about Ethan and this woman.

I wanted a divorce. He was embarrassing me. I felt strongly that I had proof of his infidelity. My daughter told me that they slept in the same bed with the door shut. That was all the proof I needed. I went to my father and shared the feelings in my heart. It hurt me deeply when Daddy told me to wait and let God do it. I said, "Wait? What more could I be waiting for? He is making a fool of me."

My daddy looked me in the eyes and said, "I would never tell you anything that would hurt you; just trust God. He is working."

Ethan kept my daughter more during this time than ever. He called and shared that he and his girlfriend were going to the fair in the city in which my parents live, and he wanted to take our daughter. It really hurt me, because every year my father gave Ethan's children money to go to the fair. Their mother and I would take them, because Ethan would never go. God pulled on my heart to let my daughter go. I didn't want to, but I obeyed. My daughter knew that all of this was hurting me so much that she said nothing about this trip.

I met her father to pick her up, and my daughter and I headed to church. As I headed to my car immediately following service, one of the church mothers pulled me aside. She said, "I saw your daughter out eating with her daddy this weekend." As she looked at me, I was embarrassed, because I knew she and several of my other church members saw him out with that other woman. I couldn't understand why he had to bring that to my new home and shame me this way. When I spoke with my daughter about it, she acknowledged that she saw them, and she did not say anything else.

I ran home to tell my daddy. I wanted him to give me permission to file for a divorce. My daddy encouraged (begged) me to let God work. I made an appointment with a lawyer the next day, though. I wanted some legal advice. I told my boss what I was doing, and he gave me permission to leave work a few minutes early to make my appointment. The next day at work, he handed me a sheet of paper titled "Thus saith the Lord on Marriage." It was complete with scriptures. He told me to go home and study and read every word that the Bible says about divorce and marriage.

I immediately went home and broke open the Bible. It took me three hours to read and dissect that Word. When I was finished, God pricked my heart. I was ashamed of myself for trying to help Him out. I interpreted the Word of God to say the following:

1. If I filed for a divorce and remarried, I could be committing adultery. Even if the new husband had never married, I would cause him to commit adultery, because he would be marrying another man's wife, in God's eyes.
2. God never intended divorce for Christians.
3. If an unbelieving husband (Ethan) put away his believing wife, then she is no longer bound.

It was clear to me what my father was trying so hard to get me to see. He wanted me to be right in God's eyes. I lost that attorney's phone number. I never called her again.

I decided to find my daughter and myself a new place to live. My mother kept her home spotless. I'm neat, but not as neat as she is. I knew that she would never complain, but she didn't like our things everywhere. We didn't either. We needed our own space. I found an apartment. I did not have any furniture. All that we owned was our clothes. My parents gave me a bedroom set. A good friend of mine gave me a living room set. I bought my daughter a new bedroom set. I also bought a kitchen table and chair set and a big screen television. It did not take my daughter and me long to fill up that apartment. My parents, sister, brother, sister-in-law, and brother-in-law helped us to move.

Life was hard. I had some bad days and some good days. I spent many days crying. I cried the whole time that I moved. My daddy told me that if I wanted to change my mind, they would support my decision. God told me that my life with Ethan was over. I knew that I was making the right decision. More than anything, I trusted God.

One day Ethan told me that he would file for a divorce himself. I know that he was worried that I would try to get money out of him for child support. His new girlfriend was also putting pressure on him. I could feel her worry that he and I might get back together. I kept telling Ethan that I should be the least of her worries. I could not physically or mentally take any more of him. I knew that it would take God Himself to tell me to go back.

I received a set of divorce papers in the mail from Ethan. I had my pen ready to sign as I read over them. I saw a line that stated, "Because of his liberal visitation with our daughter, he would pay no child support." I almost choked. I called him, and I told him that I refused to sign that paper and that he could not take away what was rightfully due our child. I did not make her on my own. It was his duty to support her financially. He and I quickly came to an agreement on child support. He sent the new papers, and I signed them. Our divorce was final on September 7, 2007. I was free in every way.

Even though I was free of him, I was still very angry and bitter toward him. I talked about what he did to me with anyone who would listen. God told me that He was going to heal my heart. I thought my heart was fine. I know that God knew better.

One day I was at my parents' house doing the usual, talking about what Ethan had put me through. I told my daddy that I would never trust another man again. I proclaimed how I did not have anything left to give anyone. Ethan stripped me of my ability to love. My daddy looked at me and said, "That is not true. You will love again. You will be so happy. God is going to send you someone, and he will love you and your daughter the way that you deserve to be loved." He also told me that when this mystery man came along, I would know that he was the one. Daddy knew how to get me out of there. I started gathering my things and invented a reason to leave. I didn't part my mouth in the presence of my father.

Like I had done in my teenage years, I fussed all the way to the car. I said to God, "If I ever trust enough to marry again, You will have to show him to me before he says a word to me." I had little confidence in anyone with my heart. More than anything or anyone, I trust God. I didn't understand why my daddy would say that to me. I didn't want to love. The last time I did, it hurt me badly. I could not entertain the thought of ever taking a chance of feeling that kind of pain again.

Deep down, I knew that what my daddy said would come to pass. In my entire life, he never told me anything wrong. I did not feel that I deserved to be happy, though. I told myself that I should have listened to everyone. I should have never married Ethan. I brought all of that on myself. I did not feel worthy of happiness, because of the bad choices that I made in the past. I went home and wallowed in self-pity.

I spent a great deal of time dwelling on what I had been through. I rehearsed it over and over and over again. I began to seek God about helping me put it behind me. God spoke a Word over me. That Word was *forgiveness*. I believed in the power of faith. I woke up the next morning and made a phone call. I called Ethan and said three words. I said, "I forgive you." For a moment he was speechless. He then wanted an explanation. I knew that I had wasted enough time and energy on him. It was time for me to be happy with me. I felt much better and much peace. I wasn't angry anymore. I claimed that God healed my heart.

I was always faithful to church. I got so much enjoyment out of going. My daughter and I did not miss a service. I watched her flourish. She came out of the shell that she had been in for so long. She laughed and smiled all of the time. She was happy to share my home with me. We were around family and people who loved us. She did not have to live life walking on eggshells anymore. She could enjoy being a child. I wanted so much for my daughter to have the life that I did, growing up in the house with her mother and her father.

    I knew that we were in the right place. At the age that she was when we left, her memories of the abuse and drama would eventually fade away. With God's help, those things would not have a negative impact on her life. I continued to buy her things and give her whatever she wanted. God revealed to me that I was not making wise decisions as her primary parent. I was creating a little monster. When I began to see my mistakes, I cut back, which was a struggle with a child used to getting her way. I truly needed God's help.

    Ethan was not being a father to her at all. He was bitter about the way that things turned out with us. After their last visit to the fair, it was the day after Christmas before he called our daughter again. We spent Christmas visiting my sister out of town. My entire family took the trip. My daughter opened her toys and appeared to be having a good day. By 6:00 in the evening, she looked at me and said, " Mama, I thought my daddy would call me on Christmas." As I looked at the disappointment in her eyes, I held back my tears. That is when I knew that even though I forgave Ethan, he could still get to me when he hurt my child. I took my family's advice and did everything in my power not to discredit him in her eyes. It became my mission to make sure that I did not influence her to see her father in a negative way. She missed her daddy. She told me that he forgot about her. Seeing her pain truly hurt me. I prayed that God help her to heal also. She did not ask for any of this. She was born with two parents.Out of nowhere, due to unforeseen circumstances, one appeared to be gone. She did not understand. There was nothing that I could do to help her to understand. I spent months trying to love the pain away. Every time that I looked in her eyes, I saw it. I was happy with life.

Seeing my daughter hurting was the only sense of unhappiness that I felt. I knew that she was blaming herself. She did not talk about it, and neither did I. The mention of her daddy became less and less often. After a while, she stopped mentioning him at all. Out of the blue, he called and wanted her to spend the night with him. At the time, my God son was visiting, so my daughter told me that she did not want to go with her daddy. I called and told Ethan about the situation. He opted to get her another time. As God took the pain away from her, He took away the desire to be with her daddy.

God used a missionary at my church to speak a Word over my life. She told me that God showed me to her, and I was very happy. I cried tears of joy all the time. She said," God has someone special for you and your little girl. You will be so happy."

I told her, "I am already happy. I don't need anyone or anything."

She said, "It is not about what you need; it is what He will do for you."

I received the message, because I knew her relationship with God. I was very scared of *love*. Life was normal for my daughter and me. We were content with it being just the two of us.

As I looked into the audience from the choir stand, his and my eyes frequently met. I ignored it. He always spoke to me after church, and I spoke in return or vice versa. I acknowledged that I must be attracted to this young man, because he caught my attention so often. It had been so long since I felt that way. I really didn't remember ever feeling butterflies in my stomach in someone's presence. This behavior continued for almost five months.

After the second month, I rebuked the devil. I said that I would never love again. I was convinced that the devil was putting this young man on my mind. As he walked in church one Sunday, I looked at him, and I asked myself, "Could he be the one that everyone keeps speaking of?" I answered myself by saying, "Couldn't be."

I heard God ask clearly, "Why not?"

I rehearsed the reasons why not over and over in my mind. He was younger than me. I had been married before, and I have a child. He did not have any children or a previous wife. A few years prior, I noticed that he was a very well-mannered young man. He came from a good family. I knew back then that he would make someone a good husband and an exceptional father. I tried to fix him up with a young woman at my church, a beautiful person, inside and out. I truly thought that they would make a great couple. Things between the two of them didn't seem to go anywhere. That was the main reason that I argued that he couldn't be the one for me.

A few Sundays later, he and I walked right into each other. As usual, he said hello, and so did I. As we began to engage in a conversation, I heard the God say, "It is not time!" I learned from my past to obey God when He speaks. I dropped everything in my hands and I walked away. As I went to my car, God began to speak. He said, "You needed me to show him to you, in order for you to believe, so that is what I did. You will know when the time is right."

He and I continued to see each other at church week after week. We never said a word to each other. I went my way, and he went his. My mother always taught us that a man should come to a woman, and a woman must stay hidden to be found. I ignored him, as if he were not there.

One particular Sunday out of the blue, his younger brother invited me to a gathering for his own birthday. As the younger brother and I stood talking, along came the young man. As his younger brother walked away, he and I continued to talk. He talked about giving the younger brother a good birthday celebration. I shared that his brother was planning his own get-together. He had just invited me.

The young man said, "I might try to do more for him."

I said, "If you need some help, let me know. Your brother has my number."

He said, "Why don't you give me your number yourself. I'd rather have it from you."

At that point I was so blown away, I didn't know what exactly to say. I gave him my phone number. I left church, and so did he. I didn't hear from him all week. He waited until seven days later to call me. As I was leaving class the following Saturday, my phone rang, and it was him. We talked for a few minutes. He shared that he was out of town visiting a friend. I told him that he could call me when he returned. I was excited to hear from him. I couldn't let him know.

We both attended his younger brother's birthday gathering. We were around each other the entire evening. Nothing had ever felt so right. We fit together just like a puzzle. After that evening, there was never a day that we did not talk.

There was one thing that truly bothered me. I quite frequently spoke to him about it. I did not want our friendship to go any further, if the young woman that I had previously tried to fix him up with did not approve.

He was such a gentleman that he volunteered to speak to her about it, if that would make me feel better. I told him that she and I were friends. It was something that I needed to do alone. I called her one evening after work. We talked for quite a while. I shared with her that he and I had been talking on the phone. We had become good friends. We had not been on a date or anything. I gave her my word that we would not proceed any further without her blessing.

She was such a sweet young woman. She immediately spoke nothing but good things of him and me. She expressed that their friendship was in years past, and if they were meant to be, it would have happened then. She encouraged both of us to be happy and be blessed.

We were ready to start going on dates. He told me that he wanted to obtain my father's permission before taking me out. He went to my father's house to talk to him about me. While sweating bullets, he asked my father's permission to date me. My father gave us his permission. I believe that my father was honored that he asked. I was very happy.

For the longest time, we did not speak to one another at church. After a while, we could not hide the fact that we had feelings for one another. Anyone around us could see it. Many of my church members gave us their blessings and well wishes. Many of them expressed how nice it was to see a couple dating the Christian way. At the same time, I could see that many others were displeased with the thought of the two of us being a couple. I could feel the cold looks. I could hear them talking about me. At first I was hoping the feeling I was getting was all in my mind.

One day I received a phone call from someone who was a former member of my church. That person asked, "What is going on?" The person wanted to know why some of the members were so disgruntled about this young man and me dating. I was told that the following things were being said about me:

1. I should get somewhere and sit down and get saved.
2. I should stop shouting and praising God all the time; I'm not saved.
3. I'm making my father look bad.
4. I've been married before and I have a child; I should suffer for the choices I made back then.
5. I should give another young woman a chance to be happy and be with him.
6. I messed up my life. I don't deserve to be with such a nice young man.

The part that hurt the most was I felt some of those things being said about me were true. I also knew who said them. I could feel it when the people looked at us together. I had already heard them talking. They were in their homes and on their jobs, talking with whomever would listen. I could hear them.

When I went to church, I continued to give God praise right in the midst of those people who were speaking so much doom about me and over my life. God hadn't done anything to me except love me and bless me. I was not going to punish Him and stop coming. The more the people talked negatively about me, the more God blessed me. The hardest part was that I had to finally pass this test and deal with this on my own. I couldn't tell my parents, and I especially couldn't tell the young man. It hurt badly.

I found strength in praising God. I praised Him every time I went to church. God made me strong. After a while, the young man sensed that something was wrong. He told me that he felt that people at church were not happy that we are dating. I told him not to worry about it. He felt that people had a problem with him. He was sure that they didn't feel that he was good enough for me, since I am the pastor's daughter.

This was so hard for me. God was leading me not to tell him all of the negative things that were being said. It tore me apart to see him beating himself up, thinking that people had a problem with him. The problem was not with him. It was with me. I tried with everything in me to encourage him. We discussed discontinuing our relationship on several occasions.

The church was getting ready to go on our bi-annual trip. I was excited because I could take a break from everything and get a little rest. His family was having a family reunion the same weekend. They did not go on the church trip.

I had a great time on the way there. I love bus rides. I slept, ate, and listened to my favorite CDs. The visiting church was always good to us. The members planned a big picnic for us. Someone came to me while I was sitting at the table enjoying the fresh air. I was told that a very close friend of my family had some cruel things to say about me dating the nice young man at church. I've known this individual since I was a little girl. I assumed that they would want to see me happy. As I listened to all that was said, I went numb. I fell into a state of depression. The devil always attacks when you are not on guard. I was relaxing and enjoying my trip. I did not expect this. I held back the tears all day long. I couldn't wait to get back to my hotel room. After the picnic, all the young people wanted to hang out and have fun. I wanted to stay in my room, alone, and in the dark. I just wanted to be left alone. I didn't understand why people who knew me all my life wanted to see me unhappy. I was hurting badly. I just lay in the bed and cried. My sister came into the room several times, trying to get me to get up. I didn't have the strength to move. My roommate was upset with me. We were looking forward to going out of town and having such a good time. She said that I was being antisocial. I still wouldn't get out of bed. The nice young man called several times, I didn't want to talk to anyone.

My sister went and told my mother that I was really in a bad state. My mother called me to come to her room. I mustered up enough energy to walk down the hallway. When I made it to her room, I lay on her couch and continued to cry. It hurt badly as I shared with my mother what happened. I don't think that it was totally what the person told me. It was a combination of things. I had been hearing things and dealing with them all by myself for so long that this was the last straw. I just couldn't take anymore.

My mother is an encourager. She talked to me for hours. I was so depressed that I just could not shake it. I went back to my room and went to sleep for the night. I gathered enough energy to get up to go to church the next morning. As I was sitting in church, the devil spoke to me and told me to end it all. My roommate had some pills lying beside the bed so I thought, "Here's my opportunity. But then there's my little girl," I thought. "What will she do without her mother?" I carefully planned what I would do. We were not leaving until the next morning. I knew that everyone would be hanging out again; therefore my room would be empty. I would use a quarter of a cup of a favored drink and dissolve those pills. I would tell my baby that she and Mommy must take the medicine for our allergies. She and I would take a nap and sleep our way off earth. I would feel no more pain. I wouldn't hear my church members talking about me anymore. I would really be free. I wouldn't have to worry about Ethan raising our daughter and inflicting the pain that he caused me on her. I had the answer; she would go with me. I couldn't leave her here on earth to deal with the fact that her mother took her life and left her. I couldn't hurt her that way. This has to be the right thing to do. I thought about the nice young man back home. How would he feel about my doing this? Then I thought, "Oh, well, once he realizes what I have been enduring from people; he will understand that life is tough and I did what I had to do to make the pain stop."

As I sat in church, my plan for the evening periodically crossed my mind. That is when it happened. The guest pastor gave his text, and it was titled "Looking for Jesus." As he preached, I knew that he was talking to me. I stood up for him the entire time as he spoke. I also cried the entire time. A young woman in the audience cried with me, and she even brought me some tissue to wipe away my tears. It felt as though she felt the pain that I was feeling. God used his manservant to get a Word to me. That Word from God saved my daughter's life and mine.

As we traveled home on the bus, I felt a whole lot stronger. The nice young man and I accepted the fact that God was drawing us together. We prayed and rebuked every devil that sought to destroy us. We made a decision to stay together. We were determined that we would do things the right way. The devil got angry. Temptation quickly arrived. The more time that passed, the stronger the feelings grew between us. He made a personal vow to live saved years before I came into his life. At that time, he also promised God that he would wait for his wife. Little did he know that I made God a very similar promise: I would not be with a man while unmarried. I don't know if it was harder for him or me. I just know that it was not easy. He did a lot of praying, and so did I. On many visits, I felt like we were in church. We prayed, read the Word, and he took a text. God kept him and me. It was a struggle, sometimes, but we made it. For that, we give all glory to God. Quite often I thanked God for my little girl. She was my inspiration during that time. I had to set a good example for her. If I did not want her to repeat my actions, I had to watch my every move.

A very good friend of mine called and told me about a miracle that God worked in her life. She shared how she truly understands how people pick up and praise God just because of how good He is. Her testimony touched me deeply, because I had prayed that God give her and several others an experience like that.

I always praise God so much because of how good He is. The thought crossed my mind, "God, the last time that I had one of those miraculous moments was when you blessed me to be hired at my new job." I was hired in an administrative position when I had never worked for the company before. That in itself was a miracle. God spoke to me and said, "While you are off work, you should go to noonday prayer at church." I obeyed, and I went to prayer that Friday.

The nice young man told me that we would be celebrating our one-year anniversary of dating on the following Saturday of the next week. He told me to be ready that evening at 6:15. God impressed upon my heart to prepare. I started getting my outfit together that Wednesday evening. I know I tried on fifty outfits, leading up to Saturday. I finally found the right one. When he arrived to pick me up, he had on black pants and a white sweater vest. I was dressed in white pants and a black shirt. The design on my pants was almost identical to the design on his tie. We matched from head to toe, and we did not previously plan our outfits. I looked at him and said, "If I forget to tell you later, I had a great time tonight." He looked back at me and smiled.

We later arrived at one of the top restaurants in the city. It is by far the nicest restaurant that I have ever been to. When I walked in, a waitress greeted me by saying, "Happy One-Year Anniversary!" All the employees of this place were dressed in black. Everyone knew that we were celebrating a year of dating. I felt very special. He let me choose our meal. We both had steak, macaroni and cheese, and a baked potato. He looked directly into my eyes while we were waiting for our food and said, "This has been a wonderful year. I love you."

I said, "I love you too; you are going to have me crying tonight."

We finished our meal, and we were on our way to the next destination. He told me, "You always say you've never been on the riverfront, so we are going downtown to look across the river.

I thought, "It is cold," but I said to him, "Okay, let's go."

We drove on the interstate and exited beside the river. He drove around and looked for a place to stop. He stopped in an area and got out to find a place for us to sit and talk. He came back to the car to get me. He brought me to the place that he found for us. He sat right beside me on a stone bench. He looked at me and asked, "How much do you love me?"

I answered, "A whole lot. How much do you love me?"

He got down on one knee and said, "So much that I want to ask you to be my wife." I was so speechless that I could not speak. He asked again, "Will you be my wife?"

I said, "Yes!" I gave him a great big hug. On that night, March 21, 2009, at approximately 8:45 p.m., he made me the happiest woman in the world. I said, "Did you, did you, ask my father?"

He said, "Already done, a month ago."

I said, "Do your parents know?"

He said, "Of course! They are the only ones who knew that tonight would be the night."

I had many questions. I wanted to know all the details. We sat and talked, and he filled in all the blanks. He completely surprised me! He swept me off my feet. I felt like a princess sitting next to my prince charming.

Seven months later, he made me his bride. We had a royal wedding. There were so many bridesmaids and groomsmen that we covered the entire altar. All of our closest friends and family were a part of our special day. The church was completely filled. God's glory shined that day and filled the room. I had dreamed about that moment all my life.

◄ J. JACKSON

He is the man of my dreams. He stands six feet, four inches tall. He weighs a little over two hundred pounds. He is tall, dark, and handsome. Not only is he good looking, he also has a heart of gold. I thank God for keeping him for me.

To the Readers of My Story

Writing this book and telling the story of my life is one of the hardest things that I have ever done. I am ashamed and embarrassed by many of the choices that I made. I know that nothing happens unless God allows it. If nothing else, God knew that you would be reading this book today. It is important to seek God in every decision and facet of your life. Your life, like mine, has already been predestined. The timing and path that you take to get to what God has for you depends on you.

God allowed the devil to take a glimpse into my future. Maybe the devil has looked into yours. You read about all the obstacles and traps the devil set in my path. In the midst of all of that, God saved my blessing of true love for me.

Many people miss their blessings. Many people do not live to see true happiness. Several women lost their lives to domestic violence during the same timeframe that I was involved in domestic abuse.

Life is all about choices. If I had any idea about my prince charming, I would have waited thirty-one years for him. I wouldn't have looked at another man before him. God allowed me to go through everything that I did for a reason. If nothing else, that reason is YOU.

I'm thankful that God chose me. I would not be who I am, if it were not for my struggles. I did not think that I would survive many of them. I don't wish what I experienced on anyone. The devil tried to destroy my mind.

It is with the mind that I serve God. Learn from my mistakes. Always choose what is right. Write your own vision. Listen to the voice of God and let Him lead you. If you cannot hear Him, go to where He is. Go to church every time the doors open. I believe that when saints gather together in His name, He will be in the midst. I hope that something I said in this book will help you along the way. Stay with the church. Stay with God; He will lead you to your destiny.

I Love You Grandma

I was twenty-two years old when God called you home. You were such a special lady. Your life touched so many people. Your death was a very tough time in my life. For as long as I can remember you were there for our family. As a child, you encouraged me to be all that I can be. You would always tell me how special I was. You told me that you knew that I would grow up to do great things. I thank God that He blessed me to have you as a grandmother. You inspired me to want to make a difference with my life. I know that you would be proud of my decision to tell my story. My daughter did not have a chance to meet you. She knows all about you. I love sharing with her my wonderful memories.. You will always live on in our hearts.

I Love You Granny

You were there for every significant event in my life cheering me on. Your smile lit up any room. Your laughter was such a beautiful sound that it caused others to join you in laughter. You had such a big heart. You loved all of us more than yourself. God called you home in 2009. I never imagined that you would ever leave this world. I will never forget how empty I felt the day you passed. Everyday is a little easier. I know that you are in a better place and you don't have to suffer or hurt anymore. I will always remember our talks. You never said a word the entire time that I experienced that horrible ordeal. As soon as God delivered me, you made me aware that you were praying for me the entire time. We laughed and talked about things that I had spent so much time crying about in the past. For as long as I live I will never forget you. I miss you so much. My life was blessed having you as my grandmother.

CPSIA information can be obtained
at www.ICGtesting.com
Printed in the USA
LVOW11s0825171216
517705LV00002B/567/P